SAINT LAURA

A NOVEL

KATE FITZGERALD

For Mother Kris

So she will walk on down that road, with her back so straight in that old green coat, the strap of her handbag pushed back all the way to the elbow, thinking how much I have cost her and never remember the days when we were two throats and one eye and we had no price.

- TONI MORRISSON, SULA

Everything she said and did was new to me, even the way she talked and the words she used, her ideas and games and the folklore that I didn't think of as folklore but as truth rumours passed from one person to another.

- JANET FRAME, TO THE IS-LAND

Only one antagonist...only one enemy...

- SHIRLEY JACKSON, HANGSAMAN

1 / SEMPER BUFO

Cane toads hibernate in the winter. They hide in damp crevices in a sleep of fury until summer, the evil season, when they come out at night to feed. When I was four years old I uncovered one of these beasts beneath a shallow layer of dirt in the back garden. I was not attempting to eat any soil — just tearing apart a few dead leaves, crushing them to dust between a chubby thumb and forefinger. The cane toad — its hateful eyes and poisonous glands — broke something in my mind. Slowly, at first. Until I reached adolescence, when those eyes grew wider and wider. I have since found it impossible to convince myself I should be alive.

My first psychiatrist was a murderer. On my first visit, I told him about my fear of cane toads.

'Their mating call sounds like a death rattle,' I said, arms crossed over my chest.

'Do you usually associate mating with death?' Doctor Brunner smirked. He had a bald, bony head and permanently raised eyebrows.

'My father says that when he was a child he saw one the size of a dinner plate and its skin was so tough that when his mother tried to chop it in half with the edge of a shovel it barely made a dent.'

'And you believe that story?'

'Yes, I believe in internal bleeding. The first blow must have done some damage. The second blow was the kill-shot.'

There was no air-conditioning in Doctor Brunner's office. He sat there, bored and unaffected by the January heat but I was endlessly wiping sweat from my upper lip, feeling it run down the back of my legs. I couldn't keep my eyes off the absurd family portrait mounted on the wall behind his desk. Taken at his son's university graduation, the boy could easily be cast as a member of the Von Trapp family. His equally blonde sister in her floral sundress gripped her brother's arm with a kind of elated urgency. Behind her stood Brunner's wife (also a therapist, I assumed) large glasses, head tilted at an angle that made her look like the editor of *Women's Weekly*; half-hearted sympathy. Doctor Brunner had a hand on his son's shoulder and was smiling. With teeth.

'Your mother tells me your father has similar problems.' The Brunner family patriarch clicked the end of his retractable pen. When we arrived at the clinic he had asked to speak to Mother Ann first (I call her this because, despite our differences, I do believe she is deserving of canonisation). My malaise needed to be corroborated. Doctor Brunner needed to know I wasn't lying. Because if I was, clearly everything was absolutely fine.

'Which problems do you mean?' Doctor Brunner shrugged and remained silent. 'You mean the toad-phobia? Cane toads are a problem for anyone. Nan — that's my father's mother, is afraid — no, she's not afraid, more distrustful of reptiles, amphibians. People too. Still didn't stop her from killing that toad.' I paused and took a giant gulp of water from the plastic bottle at my feet, wishing it was vodka. 'I'm thinking that maybe, all I want is to learn how to kill the toad. For good.'

'What interests you about that photograph? he asked, giving no sign that he was listening to anything I'd just said.

'It's behind your head. It should be facing you.'

'And why is that?'

'Why would you have a picture of your family behind your head where you can't see it?' I knew perfectly well why. He wanted to make his patients resentful of his stable and affluent nuclear family. 'It just seems wrong.'

'Then why focus on it?'

'It's behind your head, I always look behind someone's head when

I'm talking to them.'

Doctor Brunner sneered and made me fill out a tediously long questionnaire. The same question written over and over again:

1. Are you fearful all the time?
2. Are you worried something terrible might happen?
3. Do you feel like those around you may hurt you?
4. Do you feel worthless?
5. Do you feel tired?
6. Do you eat too much?
7. Do you eat too little?
8. Did your mother have these symptoms?
9. Did your father have these symptoms?
10. Did he? — Well, *did he?*

My medication was doubled.

On my second visit, I asked Doctor Brunner to fill out a form to prove I had 'enough wrong with me' to get a disability pension.

'Don't worry, Alberta,' he laughed, 'there are many, many things wrong with you.' His family in their minimalist pine frame all seemed to throw back their heads and join him.

After twenty-four hours on this new cocktail I wrote a list of things that look like Doctor Brunner:

1. *a grinning skull*
2. *a castrated bull*
3. *a Chinese finger trap*
4. *that guy from The Hills Have Eyes*
5. *a naked mole-rat.*

I made a pathetic attempt to drown myself in the bathtub. I drank three bottles of cheap chardonnay and swallowed twice the recommended dose of everything I had been prescribed. I did this in the middle of the day when no one was home and slipped, limp and determined, under the water. The water was green from pine scented bath salts and it was like I was falling asleep in a wet forest cave filled with moss and leeches crawling up my thick, hairy tree-trunk legs. I let the air drain from my lungs and fill with water until the pain set in and I surfaced — violently coughing; my breathing quick and shallow. Half the bathwater ended up on the floor. Some ran under the door.

On my third visit to Doctor Brunner, he tested my reading speed. I told him my thoughts wouldn't stop, that they raced about my head and I couldn't sleep. I kept recalling things others had said and I repeated them to myself in a manner that was much more vicious.

He asked me to read from a bland history of the hot air balloon. I read very fast, he said, I slurred many of my words (I was nervous, I was in public, I was exhausted, I was embarrassed). This was part of his ongoing research into Attention Deficit Disorder, he informed me. He offered me a prescription for mood stabilisers and quite a high dose of dexamphetamine. I wasn't allowed any benzodiazepines, that would be too much of a crutch, make me feel too human, and offer sleep without violent dreams. I don't understand why Mother Ann can get a prescription of benzos without any questions but it's off limits to people like me who actually need it.

Two months later, one of Doctor Brunner's patients drove headlong into another car on the freeway. She killed herself and a family of five. She was found to have ten times the legal dosage of dexamphetamine in her system. Sometimes I think she might have seen Mister San Hosantio (her version of him) walk into the middle of the road, maybe he took the wheel, like Jesus. Her family will see Doctor Brunner in court, the papers said.

Cane toads. Every encounter I have had with them since that day in the garden has heralded a disaster. Or, at least, some kind of change. I am currently nineteen years old. I spend a lot of time asleep. I finished high school and went to bed, with only a few futile attempts at beginning life as an adult, amid a haze of exhaustion and sadness. I live with Mother Ann and my brother, Louis. Here, we never get a proper winter. I know I will never see snow. Our garden is overgrown and full of bush turkeys. I have a dog called Camille. She is half Labrador, half Border Collie. Once a group of kids rode past on their bikes while Camille and I were sitting in the front garden and one of them yelled: 'Everyone in your house is fat! Even the dog is fat!'

Because of my perpetual guilt regarding the burden I place on my mother, I make an extra effort to help her out. I contribute to the housework and pay board from my pension – Doctor Brunner's misdiagnoses had at least come through for me there. This debilitating state I am in is often not seen as debilitating enough in the eyes of civil servants. You must be missing a limb or excreting bodily fluids in public. They must see that your brain is sick. You must look like you can't look after yourself, which means they expect you to be in a continuous state of psychosis. For example, some days I am too weak to take the bins out. When I can manage it, I run the risk of being accused of lying about the times I couldn't. I should have stopped doing it altogether because once, at sundown, a toad jumped across my foot as I was dragging them down our long, gravel driveway. I was too tired to wear shoes, every muscle ached from tensing during the nightmares so the little extra pain of sharp gravel under my feet didn't make much difference.

I spent my first seven years in an affordable weatherboard hotbox in the northern end of the city. Next door was the Pigeon Club, a modest building set in the immediate centre of a bland half-acreage that was mown by an old man in a bucket hat every day without fail. No trees, not even a fence existed to complement the Pigeon Club. It stood out like a portent of misery, a mystifying crest of arms above the door. I assumed it was a place for pigeon enthusiasts to meet and talk birds, but it was later explained to me by my father (Father Robert — not as deserving of canonisation but the formal nature of the title is fitting) that the place was indeed 'quite masonic' – just a little apron and ring-wearing, as opposed to 'very masonic' which, I guess, involves having a hand in upsetting the balance of global power.

I took a few ballet classes at the Pigeon Club with a few girls I knew from school. The teacher's name was Roz. She was tired and impatient. She smelled of cigarettes and crushed resin. She scolded me for using my arms inappropriately.

'Alberta, we are not playing windmills,' she shouted.

'Stop playing horrid,' I responded, like a post-war boarding school girl.

'You'll never end up in points with that attitude, Miss.' As though binding and crippling my toes was the endgame.

I ran home. I wish it was still so easy to just run next door to your bed when the world is playing horrid.

2 / A RESURRECTION, A STAIN

The amount of time between the altercation with Roz at the Pigeon Club and our move to the country seems instantaneous but it would be another two years before we moved away from the city. A blur of a hallway, I can't remember which door led where. My bedroom floor covered in Little Golden Books, their cardboard covers gnawed by tiny teeth. A white chest of drawers lined with re-purposed wrapping paper covered in Mr Men (Mr Bump was my favourite. He was a walking wound); the kitchen, a mess of orange laminate. The boy next door, his parents were doctors, they owned a pool. He had curly blond hair like a sanitised Disney Cupid, and he would point and shout: 'Mad! that's the mad girl.' Cupid thinks I am mad. Best leave all that behind. I didn't have anyone I would call a friend at school, but I suspect that when you are very young it's difficult to understand the concept of friendship. All I did for my first few years was exist alongside other children. It didn't really matter from one day to the next who was sitting beside me and any petty quarrel that occurred would be forgotten the next day.

My clearest memory from that time was a car journey north. I was seven. It was the last month of the nineteen eighties. A steep winding road, a change in altitude, I was given a barley sugar to suck, my ears were blocked and it was only when we reached the top of the mountain that I yawned and swallowed and swallowed again and they crackled clear like an old ham radio.

I recall sitting in front of a strange television. A wooden lever where the dials should be. I informed Mother Ann that we already had a television.

'Silly girl. It's a fireplace,' she replied. *Silly girl, why worry about such things, silly girl, breathe in and out, silly girl why would you think that? Silly girl.* I'd only seen the kind of fireplaces that were ornate and intimidating, open with a mantelpiece on which one displayed toby jugs, wedding portraits and chrysanthemums. Maybe the ashes of a dead relative. I'd never seen anything like this dull metal box with a chimney that looked like an alien probe, silver and full of holes. Clinical and stale.

On the first day in our new house I bit Louis. Hard, on the forearm. A small amount of blood was drawn. We were to share a bedroom until we could afford to build an extension to this ugly kit home with a skylight, weatherboard, painted a dark green. The pointy painted box. I didn't understand the point of the wedge-shaped skylight on the roof. I bit my brother because he wouldn't let me put my collection of Sylvanian Families on the empty shelf at the foot of his bed. He screamed and started slapping me so hard and fast it was difficult to tell where his limbs began and ended. A sharp sting repeating across my back.

'It's mine, it's mine, give it back to me!' he screeched, throwing Boris, the patriarch of the Brown Bear family, across the room.

Louis is two years younger than me and could, even at the age of five, overpower me in a physical altercation. I was usually the one that started it, or so family lore would have it. Doctors and specialists and other vermin had told my mother that Louis would never look her in the eye, never show affection, never function as a normal member of society. I heard her crying through the thin walls of our new affordable hotbox the night of Louis' diagnosis. I heard a low mumble from my father, likely doing a terrible job of comforting her. A low mumble was all I ever heard from Father Robert. Communication failed him in times of great import. He never raised his voice. Mother Ann and I were far too shrill for him. Too excitable. He would say odd things like: 'Keep that music down, all the neighbours will hear and think we're Philistines.' Father Robert only listens to Mahler symphonies.

Mother Ann realised early on I was not going to be her saving grace, her cornerstone of sanity. Especially when I bit Louis and said:

'He did it himself because he hates me and look, I have bitten myself as well because I hate me, I don't hate him I hate me, look — look!'

She was too busy comforting Louis to notice the pathetic hickey I had given myself on the inside of my arm. I remember studying the self-inflicted bruise; purple and yellow surrounding the red, rash-like spots while Mother Ann shouted at Father Robert to get Louis' colic tablets. Louis was kicking at the wall with his dirty feet, a gurgling scream emitting from his throat. I noticed the colours on my arm fading so I sucked at it again. When Louis had calmed and settled in front of *1,2,3 with Postman Pat*. I tried again.

'Look at what I did.'

Mother Ann turned towards me, exhausted, but shocked. She told me to never ever do it again because people would think I was disgusting and rude but wouldn't tell me why because it was something I was far too young to understand. Now I know. It means a boy will leave these all over your chest and you will think it was done out of love.

Of course, no one would believe that Louis would bite himself. He would beat his head with his hands but he would never attempt to break skin, to reach for the blade. I don't think now, after he has disproved everything those doctors said, that he wants to die like I do. He wants to draw his favourite cartoon characters and maintain exceptional knowledge of obscure children's programmes.

3 / THE HEADLESS NUN

So much time can be spent discussing a town. There was Durston's Garage, the dump, the cemetery, the sports club. That was it for us. If we needed anything else, we had to drive for half an hour to the next town over, that contained more of a semblance of sentient life. Where the farmers mixed with the upper middle class, the retirees, the Hare Krishna, the craft stores, the Country Women's Association, The Lions Club, another quite masonic club, tourists in broad-brimmed hats fellating gourmet ice cream cones and cafes and cafes and cafes.Everything came with hemp and kombucha and placenta.

Mother Ann quickly got to know a lot of people just from shopping at the local supermarket (named 'Farmhouse Legacy' boasting quality produce since 1919) and clients at the solicitor's where she worked as a receptionist. But in those days she never had any genuine friends. My father would not have it. People frightened him. No one could visit. He worried that Louis might throw a tantrum if Mother Ann invited a nice rural couple over for a cup of tea and then they would tell all their nice rural friends and before we knew it we would be chased out of town. I once overheard him say to Mother Ann that if — *if* I made some friends at my new school, they could never come and visit because they would inevitably spread rumours about him. All the possible social outcomes he could imagine were certified catastrophes. He said it was all too hard. The hardest things always fell on Father Robert.

A town of green hills. The colour of the fat tree frogs I would find clinging to my bedroom window. I don't see them so often nowadays. They are being eaten by the cane toads. For a long time I was convinced they had followed me here. I imagined they infiltrated certain areas via an interconnected network of tunnels. They say salt kills cane toads but that's a lie. Only the shovel.

Unlike ours, most houses in the area were made from real wood. Western Red Cedar. All my school friends had houses made from Western Red Cedar. No plywood. I would walk to the top of our steep driveway and sit on the side of the road. It was the narrowest road imaginable. Two passing vehicles needed to swerve wide to avoid colliding, but that rarely happened. I could sit in the grass gully by the side of the road and remain quite safe and quite anonymous. It was my version of 'running away'. Once I even tied a handkerchief full of food to a stick and slung it over my shoulder, part defiant, part miffed the hanky wasn't red with white spots, like in cartoons. I wanted to protest the ugly fireplace, the fact that Louis just tore the cover off my illustrated hardback copy of *The Wind in the Willows* and scribbled on the endpapers with a brown felt pen, defacing the only place I could find a harmless toad.

I sat on the side of the road eating an apple from my hanky and stared at the colonial style cottage across the road. It didn't need to hide like ours did, down a long driveway. It sat with its chest out — if a building could ever do such a thing, behind an immaculate hedge. One day I noticed it was up for sale. The sign read: 'For Sale. Spink & Percy Realty: Serving the Range Since 1951! Property Manager: Jan Boynahan'. In my intense surveillance of the property I hadn't ever seen anyone go in or out. Certainly, not someone that looked like their name would be Jan Boynahan. No potential buyers. Which was just as well, I thought, because I imagined the place to be haunted. Sometimes, I thought I saw the shadow of a person, a man, in one of the upstairs bay windows.

I had been thinking about ghosts a lot since Father Robert told me about the headless nun. He went to a Roman Catholic boarding school, run by sadistic brothers and severe sisters. The oldest building on the grounds was no longer used, because it was haunted by the ghost of a headless nun. There were lots of versions of the story, but the most popular one was that the nun in question was having an affair with one of the brothers and fell pregnant. To cover up his sin, the brother killed her by cutting off her head on a moonlit night at the top of the tower.

'Well that was silly of him,' I said. Silly of you, Father Robert, to confide in your seven-year-old daughter and fill her mind with such violence.

'How so?' asked Father Robert.

'The baby would still be alive in her belly.'

He explained that babies are wired up to the mother like plugging in a toaster and if the mains power explodes so does the toaster. So, if the mother is the mains and the baby is the toaster, if the nun lost her head, then so would the baby. That's how I understood it, never mind that there are easier, more subtle ways to kill someone than decapitation, but there are also many ways to lose your head. A lesson in murder and reproduction and I hadn't even begun school. A treat.

Father Robert never saw the headless nun himself, but he could see the tower from his bed in the boarding house, and he stayed awake, often for hours, too terrified to close his eyes. He said he was worried she would come in through the window, or he would find her standing at the foot of his bed. I told him she would be much scarier if she had a head. He disagreed.

'Just a body is enough. A crowd is also frightening because you don't necessarily look at the faces moving around you, it's just a crush of bodies, suffocating you.'

I wondered if he had ever told my mother this. Maybe she would understand him better. He never knew how to use his words. He often said he wouldn't mind if he never spoke again, especially when we told him he was wrong.

On a hot afternoon as I sat in my ditch, half willing the nun to appear in the window of the house across the road, I heard the squeak of a bicycle chain. A boy came riding down the street on a beaten-up old BMX. I lost my chance to run back inside, to at least get inside the gate and hide behind the bushes until he had passed. He was already slowing down. He was wearing a horse-riding helmet with a Valvoline sticker on the side, a pair of fluorescent yellow board shorts and no shirt. He was terribly sunburnt. No shoes. I curled inwards on myself, stared at my feet, my mind simultaneously blank and racing with an unidentifiable fear. A crush of bodies. Was one body enough to suffocate you? The bitumen road was hot and narrow. I saw the balls of his feet scrape across hot tar. It was the beginning of summer but the temperature was already reaching above thirty-five degrees. I looked up. The sun was behind him and the visor on the riding helmet left his face in the shadows. He demanded I tell him my name and how old I was.

'Alberta. I'm seven. Eight in July. I mean, next year I will be eight… in July.'

'I'm Hayley. I know I've got a girl's name but my mum says it's for both boys and girls and I'm nine. Ten on March the ninth. There are two girls in my grade called Hayley — they call me Boy Hayley but all the other boys say I'm a girl too.'

I didn't know where to look so I plunged my fists into my eye sockets. If there wasn't so much skin and tissue and vitreous body and optic nerve in the way, my balled-up hands would have fit snugly inside my skull. Safely held within the orbital fissure. I could tell without looking that Hayley was confused, already seeing me as a chore. As difficult. I've always been very good at sensing how people feel about me. I got up to leave but he called me back and asked me if I was starting school after Christmas. I said I was.

'I'll be in grade six. Which is lucky cause they almost kept me back. Because Mr Hayes said — he told Mum, she went all the way to this meeting at school and she said it was okay but then Dad said I'm dumb.'

'Why?'

'He just said. Are you smart?'

'I don't know.' I noticed he still had the balls of his feet planted firmly on the road. 'Do your feet hurt?' I asked.

'Nah, I've got tough feet.' Hayley took off his helmet. His dark brown hair reached his shoulders and was wet with sweat. He had the glow that belonged to a child of the outdoors. I had already seen, from the safety of my mother's car, a few of these children. They made me think of tyre swings over flowing river beds and treehouses. But at the same time, I couldn't entirely picture Hayley in any of those scenarios. The skin on his bony shoulders was peeling and there was a large weeping cut on his bottom lip. He lifted the thick dirty sole of his foot and virtually stuck it in my face. It smelled of crushed dandelions and tar.

'Asbestos feet. That's what my mum says. She can take a hot pan out of the oven without wearing gloves. Asbestos hands, she says. She doesn't make cakes anymore.' He lowered his foot and rolled a piece of loose bitumen around under his big toe.

'How did you cut your lip?' I was feeling at ease enough to ask a question.

'Was playing with Agnes. Wasn't her fault. She just got excited. That's my dog, she's crazy. Dad reckons she might have dingo in her. I named her after my grandma; she died last year but she was crazy too. Mum's still sad about it. She gets sad when I say the dog's name, Agnes, 'cause it was Grandma's name, so I've started calling her 'mongrel' because that's what Dad calls her anyway. Dad says Grandma Agnes was a mongrel too.'

The only way I ever make friends is if I am forced into it, coerced by a dominant personality. It takes very little effort on my part. Still, Hayley was somewhat of an anomaly because if he had been just a few years older when we met, he would have ridden straight past me.

He told me his father ran Durston's Garage, just around the corner. His father's name was Bill. His mother was called Helen.

'We can smell petrol from our house but you get used to it. What does your dad do?'

'Housework,' I replied. I couldn't exactly say 'hiding'. I said Mother Ann was the one who worked. As a receptionist at the solicitor's office. I asked him what his mother did for work.

'Nothing,' he shrugged. 'She used to run a shop in town, she made — makes jewellery.' He pointed to four woven bracelets that dangled from his tiny wrist. 'She's sick a lot. She gets headaches and cries and sleeps. But it's okay because we sell chips at the petrol station and I can eat as much as I want. I'll bring you some next time I come around.

Can I come and visit your house? You got any good stuff? My cousin has a huge X-Wing fighter.'

'Got a little Imperial Walker?' was all I could offer.

'You have an AT-AT? The huge one that opens up and you can keep all your stuff inside it like secret junk?'

'No. I wanted that but it's too expensive. It's an AT-ST. The one with chicken legs.'

Hayley promptly asked to visit and I wanted to say no. How did I know this boy wasn't planning a dreadful humiliation? I may have said yes. I may have said no. I may have nodded. I could have made the most inaudible of noises but Hayley must have been satisfied with my answer because he rode off in a hurry – like in films when someone is on the phone and they just hang up without saying goodbye, or order food at a restaurant and abruptly leave without eating anything. Did I just give this boy permission to show up at our door unannounced? Was I now tethered to Hayley's every chaotic whim? If so, Father Robert would break. He had taught me to hide where I couldn't be seen from the front windows if a Jehovah's witness or salesperson came knocking. Hiding was a rule – especially if Mother Ann wasn't home to handle it.

What followed was what I call 'The Year Without Laura'. A year of peace or relative naivety or solitude, or emptiness. It all depends, really. Cyclone Laura. Many farmers lost their crops the day Laura rolled into town, but at least she broke the drought. A blessing and a curse. In the Year Without Laura, Hayley knew himself. As a boy, he cared. His mother would drowsily place another bracelet on her son's wrist, a new one for every time she felt guilty, one for every time she was sorry, one for every time she wasn't awake to teach him how a man should behave. To apologise for her husband. Sometimes he would have ten on either wrist at a time. He had to retire the older ones eventually to make room for the new ones. But the first bracelet Helen Durston ever gave him always remained on his wrist, brittle and faded, brown and thin from years of sweat, labour, grief. Hayley held on to the grief of the women in his life like military stripes, even though he wasn't the one who fought the war.

'He's simple, that boy,' my father said once. Father Robert had the habit of speaking like an Edwardian schoolmaster. He learned this much about Hayley from overhearing him speak. Once. I think he mistook his sincerity for a lack of intelligence. Father Robert couldn't be sincere. He avoided calling anyone by their name. Instead he would say 'the girl', 'the boy', or 'the wife'.

4 / A CRIME

On my first day of grade three, I sobbed for an hour before I could even set foot out of the car. Mother Ann had to drive back down the street to her work — leaving the engine running and me blubbering in the backseat — to let her boss know she would be in as soon as she could get this weak, pathetic child to school. When she pulled up outside the school a second time, she managed to coax me out of the car and guide me, with a tender yet strained push, to the door of my classroom. The teacher, Ms. Bellthorpe, loomed over me. She was tall, had short, spiked hair full of gel and giant, owl-shaped glasses. As kind as her words were, she seemed threatening in comparison to Mother Ann's soft belly and blonde shoulder-length hair. Ms. Bellthorpe was wearing a red crepe pantsuit with enormous shoulder pads making her look like an inverted triangle. She was only a few years out of teacher's college. To me, she looked forty. She was in visual opposition to Mother Ann — her favourite colour was sky blue. That day she was wearing a straight sky blue muslin skirt with white sandals. I clung to her and stared at the sandals, part of the buckle was starting to rust.

The next thing I remember is Ms. Bellthorpe's red crepe trousers, covered in pink sick and her phoning my mother and sighing a lot.

I spent the drive home with my head inside an ice cream container that Ms. Bellthorpe had given me. She had to tip out all the crayons that were inside, so I dry heaved into a chaotic rainbow debris each time Mother Ann took a sharp turn.

I was allowed a day off to get over the poisoning.

'I thought that watermelon was a bit old,' I heard Father Robert say from my bed. You can hear, and almost see, anything going on in that house if you keep all the doors open. Open plan, no upstairs, no hallways, no privacy. 'Why on earth did you give her rotten watermelon? She was already a nervous wreck.'

Mother Ann let out one of her loud, exasperated sighs.

'Well next time you can make her lunch. You are at least driving her to school from now on.'

'What will I do with Louis?'

'You take him too.'

'But I'd have to walk him to the SLC.'

This was the 'Special Learning Centre', where students with certain 'needs' were locked away in a demountable building with no air-conditioning at the bottom of the school grounds, well away from the other children for fear of contagion.

'What if he cracks up?' Father Robert moaned. 'He slapped me across the thigh with that big barbeque spatula yesterday — because, of course, how dare I admonish him for smearing his shit all over himself.'

I had heard Mother Ann talk to Ma, my grandmother, over the phone about Father Robert's 'phobias'. I thought maybe he was scared to leave the house because of spiders, or snakes, as I had identified in myself a phobia of cane toads. I'm only just starting to understand. I am a lot like him, but instead of never apologising, I apologise profusely. I have made it my duty to apologise for myself to the point of excess, especially to Mother Ann. I'm sorry for your position as a constant caregiver. I'm sorry I was inconvenient invalid number three.

Father Robert was driving around the block trying to find a park, Louis screaming in the back seat. He dropped me off in front of the school first, so at least I didn't have to walk in with them. I heard another car honk at him as he drove off. I didn't know why. But it made my stomach turn. And it turned again when from my classroom, long after the bell had rung, I heard Louis crying in the distance and I imagined Father Robert pulling him by the arm, swearing under his breath. I knew he had made Louis late on purpose.

The day was a series of stomach turns. Not in the way of nausea but of fear, insecurity, the feeling when you fall off a cliff in a dream. I don't remember any specific lessons, just staring at various tools in my hand. Some wooden blocks for counting, some flash cards with letters of the alphabet on them, more crayons. At lunch time, a girl named Philomena Rankin sat down next to me.

'You weren't here yesterday,' she said, in an accusatory tone.

'I was sick. I ate a bad watermelon.'

'Ew,' said Philomena. 'Well, you missed yesterday's lunch and that was important because we decided who goes in what group and who gets to be friends with who and stuff. So, you're not in a group. What's your name?'

I introduced myself in a guarded manner. Philomena nodded casually and began colouring in her nails with a black felt-tip pen. We weren't allowed felt-tip pens until at least grade four.

'No one picked me. They said my mum drinks bathwater which isn't true but now you're here we can be a group.'

'Okay,' I said, cautiously sniffing a granny smith apple. I was now convinced all food could be poison.

Philomena had big brown freckles across her nose like she'd drawn them on in a rush before doing her nails. She wore a stone-washed denim skirt with her school shirt, instead of the regulation pleated maroon sports skirt. I considered going to find Hayley but was scared he'd forget who I was. So I stayed with this strange mess of a girl. Hungry but nauseated at the thought of eating. Philomena suddenly got all quiet and serious:

'Psst,' she hissed. She sounded like that shady guy with the overcoat from *Sesame Street* who would try to sell Ernie contraband letters and numerals. Everything about Philomena was cheeky and impish with the slightest whiff of parental neglect. 'Psst, hey, Alberta,' she whispered again, her hand cuffed around my ear. Her breath smelled of Vegemite and crackers. 'You know those stickers Ms. Bell has? Like, those big ones with animals on them? We all got one at the end of our first day. I put mine on my head — that's a trend I started. You need one. She keeps the door to the classroom open at lunchtime. I went in yesterday, there are so many stickers in there.'

It took me longer than it should have to register we were stealing until we were standing at Ms. Bell's desk with the small metal drawer wide open, tearing lengths of round stickers from a paper roll. Philomena immediately slapped one on my forehead, so I could be de rigueur. It had a picture of a platypus on it, giving two thumbs up. Then, Ms. Bell strode through the door with a large mug in her hand. Philomena ran, nudging the teacher aside on her way out the door. Hot tea lashed onto the carpet.

Ms. Bell sighed. Placing her mug on her desk, she pulled a bunch of tissues from her jacket sleeve (this one was khaki) and dabbed at the mess on the floor.

'That Rankin girl,' she muttered. I wasn't sure if she was speaking to me or to herself. 'Bloody pain in the...' She looked up at me. 'Alberta, I don't think you should hang around with Philomena anymore. I'll let you off this time because I know this was her idea. Off you go.'

I ran off the same way Philomena had, the sprint of the juvenile delinquent, the platypus sticker still on my head. I ran to the toilets, tore the sticker off, flushed it and hid there until lunch was over. Philomena didn't return to class.

5 / DISCO INFERNO

Philomena was absent a lot, following the Great Sticker Heist of 1990. When she did show up, she pretended not to know me, like the whole incident had been my fault. I had started eating lunch with Justine Birch, a minister's daughter with golden braids who was kind but lacking in conversation and Rachael Gold, a confused, bookish girl who had a perpetual cold. Rachael and I liked to visit the library and sit on a long cushion shaped like a snake made up of random pieces of scrap material. We ploughed our way through *Meg and Mog* and *Frog and Toad*.

I blamed myself when Justine and Rachael withdrew from me. I thought maybe I hadn't tried hard enough. They kept walking off down the bottom of the playground, saying I couldn't come with them because they were conferring about what they were going to buy me for my birthday. On one such occasion when I was left alone contemplating what my gift would be, Philomena edged up to me and whispered that she knew what Justine and Rachael were talking about and it 'wasn't nice stuff.' She heard them say that my family was ashamed of Louis and kept him hidden in a cellar (I never knew anyone with a cellar) because we were ashamed of him, that I never invited people over because I slept in the bathtub (not as bad as drinking from it, I suppose).

'Even if they did get you a birthday present, your brother would just eat it,' Philomena smirked. It was the last day of class before the June holidays. I was glad of two weeks of respite.

Over the holidays, Philomena died of an aneurysm. I heard Mother Ann whispering to a work colleague that Philomena had been complaining of a headache the night before and her mother sent her to bed without any painkillers and didn't think to check on her until around three o'clock the following afternoon. I also learned that Philomena's (clearly negligent) mother had screamed and screamed at the funeral, that she had cursed Philomena's estranged father for not coming, cursed herself, her own mother, the whole town. Serves her right, everyone supposed.

This all occurred at a time when the concept of spontaneous human combustion was tossed around the playground in morbid whispers. Your organs can have a chemical reaction and boom — your brain can go on fire and make you explode. They said Philomena's burning brain exploded out of her skull and burned her bed and nothing else in the room.

Just days after Philomena was buried, a fire started in the long grass at the edge of the oval. There was an old furnace down there and we were never sure why. We had to perform a fire drill for real. Ms. Bell wore a yellow hard hat with 'Fire Lady' written on it. As we sat in our class groups in the emergency evacuation area, answering the roll call, Hayley snuck over to me and said he reckoned a kid in his grade who had a cigarette lighter tried to get the furnace going by setting fire to a bunch of twigs. But the rumour that had already started to circulate was that the ghost of Philomena Rankin had returned to immolate herself, over and over again. It thus became a common ritual to leave an offering by the old furnace. Philomena's Pyre— a lolly, a puffy sticker, a coloured pencil, a cheese slice — otherwise she would come at night to get you, her whole body black and burned, whether you said her mother drank bathwater or not.

Hayley did eventually decide to show up at my house – out of breath and unannounced. Father Robert was washing up at the kitchen window and knowing he was visible from the front door ran to the bathroom swearing under his breath. I, following suit, ran from my place on the floor in front of the TV and into my bedroom. I wasn't missing anything. I had no choice but to watch Louis rewind and fast forward and pause his favourite parts of *Fireman Sam* until the heads on the VHS player broke. Mother Ann had to clean the dirt from them, manually, with a business card covered in methylated spirits. She did this about ten times a day. We left the top cover off the VHS player permanently. Everything in our house was like that — pieces were missing, either because of Louis or to accommodate him.

Of course, when Hayley knocked on the door that Saturday morning. Louis ran to the door shouting. I hid under my bed and blocked my ears. The terrible thing that Father Robert was warning me about had occurred. I needed to disappear until it was over. I heard a few murmurs, a few sporadic shouts from Louis until I heard my bedroom door open. A bit of awkward questioning from Mother Ann followed: Did I know a boy named Hayley Durston? Who was he? Where did he live?

'He wants to know if you want to play with your toys. It's okay with me if you stay in the yard. It's a bit strange that he wants to hang around with a girl. He has a girl's name I suppose.' She giggled. I must have looked visibly upset because she immediately started apologising in an uncomfortable, vague manner, as though the thought had only just occurred to her that my name shortened, 'Albert' and the one she used the most — 'Al', were both typically male. 'I know, I know, that's a silly thing to laugh about. I just didn't know Hayley was a boy's name too.'

'His mum makes jewellery,' I said, bewildered.

Louis was shouting for Father Robert to stop hiding in the bathroom. Mother Ann, obviously trying to put an end to the whole incident, told me she would tell Hayley to go away if that's what I wanted, adding that Ma wouldn't let her hang around with boys when she was my age but he did bring his dog and she thought I might like that. I had been asking about getting a dog. Father Robert was not keen on the idea, but I knew my life would somehow improve if I had one.

'Her name is Agnes,' I said, crawling from my hiding place and fetching a large Tupperware box filled with figurines. Mother Ann suddenly seemed panicked.

'I'll keep an eye on you from inside, okay? And he can't come in.

Sorry, darling, I know it's a pain but—' she lowered her voice to a whisper, '—your father will have a heart attack.' I nodded and ran to the door where Hayley was standing behind the flyscreen scratching an insect bite on his leg while a black, rotund cattle dog simultaneously attempted to lick the offending spot. When she saw me, she jumped up and clawed the screen.

'Sorry!' he called to my mother who was standing behind me, ushering me out through a crack in the door so Agnes wouldn't slip inside.

Mother Ann forced a smile.

'Stay out the back where I can see you.'

I handed Hayley my container of toys and knelt to pat Agnes.

'Don't get too close to her bum,' Hayley said, 'because if you do, you'll smell like dog fart forever.'

I led him round to the back of the house where Father Robert had assembled a swing set for me and Louis that neither of us ever used. We didn't talk much. He sat on the grass, enthralled by my toys. It was like he'd never seen one in his life. I played with Agnes, distracting myself sufficiently so I didn't feel obliged to make conversation until Hayley announced:

'My neighbour wants to shoot Agnes.'

He explained that a man named Mr Monterey who lived across the road told his dad that if Agnes escaped into their yard and bothered their horses again he'd 'get his gun out'. When Hayley saw how visibly upset I was by this, he told a very poor lie:

'He didn't mean it, but it doesn't mean I won't bash him if he says something like that again.'

I did my best not to look distressed. But after Hayley went home and I went back inside I burst into tears in front of my parents and I couldn't tell them why. Hayley was not allowed to come over again.

Rachael started hanging around me again as a kind of unspoken apology, after Justine moved away. I was worried Hayley would show up at my house again and my family would have to replay the whole sorry affair. But he didn't. He was less comfortable associating with me at school. Being friends with a girl would clearly worsen the humiliation he already received for – in their opinion – 'looking like one'.

I was using the lack of attention paid to me at home to my advantage. I had 'run away' again (this time with a handful of almonds and chewable Vitamin C tablets inside a paper bag) when I saw Hayley's bike approaching. I wanted to run back inside, but I felt so alone I was prepared to risk the discomfort. When he saw me, he veered his bike off the road and threw it casually to the ground. He stood over me with his arms crossed like he had something of great import to discuss.

'What's in the bag?' he asked, skinned knees at eye level.

'Nuts and some medicine,' I said.

'You running away?'

I nodded.

'I can show you where to go.'

Every weekend we would explore the expansive farmland behind Hayley's house. He told me most of the land belonged to the Montereys, but he was so nonchalant about the fact that Mr Monterey had threatened to shoot Agnes that I felt silly bringing up any concerns about trespassing on his land. Mother Ann became lax in her supervision of my outdoor activities and we took advantage of days when Louis was particularly ferocious. Eventually, Hayley invited me inside his house. It sat behind Durston's Garage and wasn't visible from the road. To get there, you had to walk past the Garage, down a cul-de-sac called Solstice Lane. Hayley told me, with some pride, that his family were the only ones on Solstice Lane, that it might as well belong to them. The Durston house was a lot older than mine. White paint was peeling off all over the wooden exterior and the windows were made of an outdated, orange textured glass, cracked in many places.

We walked into the living room. The TV was playing one of those midday movies from the 1960s about surfing teenagers like *Gidget* or *Beach Blanket Bingo*. Helen Durston was lying on the couch, a wet towel over her face. Not a washer, not a hand towel, it was more like a beach towel. Or at least a bathmat. It doesn't seem important, but I wish I could remember because whatever it was seemed too heavy, like it was suffocating her. She hadn't bothered to wring it out, so water ran down her arms that hung, limp, down the side of the couch. Tiny droplets fell onto a ragged copy of a magazine. On the cover was a woman laughing heartily as she covered her bare chest with her arms next to the headline: 'Wacky Teen's Amazing Demand: Chop Off My Legs!'

'Mum?' Hayley whispered, lifting the towel gently, as though he was making sure she was still alive. The sea green colour of the towel cast a sickly glow over her face. She opened her eyes slowly and I remember her lashes, all stuck together. And the long dark hair plastered over her face.

'Migraine,' she mumbled.

'Then go to bed.' Hayley fished around for the remote control, turned the TV off and tossed the magazine under the couch like a limp frisbee.

'Who's this?' Helen sat up. She was wearing a thin nightdress with a picture of a teddy bear on it. Its arms were open wide and there was a caption underneath it in balloon lettering that read: 'I Just Wanna be Loved by You'. A strap fell from a thin shoulder.

'Hello,' I offered meekly. 'Hayley said I…'

She sat up, fixing up the strap and covering her chest with a faded tie-dyed pillow. She pushed her hair out of her eyes and rubbed her hands roughly over her face.

Hayley stammered something about my name being Alberta and that I lived down the road and had heaps of good toys. I half expected him to apologise for my presence.

Helen motioned to me to come closer to her.

'Alberta, he's only as good as he can be.'

Hayley started tugging her gently by the arm, again suggesting she to bed. I noticed she had a faded tattoo — a small black star — on her wrist.

She swatted his hand away.

'You know, you've got to just…' she picked up some sort of polished gemstone from the coffee table and started turning it over and over in her hands. '…you know?'

I nodded. A little too hard. I was too frightened to ask what she meant.

'Mum,' Hayley persisted.

'Can you both just go outside please?' she snapped, lying back down on the couch, placing her forearm theatrically over her eyes. I didn't know women had hair under their arms.

'Sorry, I'm sorry,' I said as Hayley grabbed me by the wrist and dragged me away. When we reached the kitchen I could hear Agnes scratching on the back door.

'Agnes wants to go up the paddock,' he mumbled, despondent; his head inside the rusting fridge.

There was one picture on the door of the fridge, held there with a magnet shaped like a toucan. A photograph of Helen, younger, fuller in the face, her hair waist-length and shiny under a floppy straw hat. She held a baby in her arms and she smiled, closed lipped in a way that reminded me of a photo of Linda Ronstadt on the cover of one of Mother Ann's old vinyl records. The record was called 'Silk Purse' and Linda was sitting in a pig pen but not giving a damn, looking like I hoped to look as a teenager — lithe and barefoot with hoop earrings and a ring on every finger. There is a song on that record about a man with cold evil eyes who made the sun go dark. Hayley sighed and slammed the fridge shut, making me jump slightly.

'No carrots. Jack will have to eat grass today.'

'Is that baby you?' I asked, pointing to the picture.

'Yeah. Who cares?'

The farm behind the Durston property was open pasture for about five kilometres and beyond that, thick, dry bush. Hayley said there was a creek on the other side, and then more land.

It seems, when you're only small and navigating a large expanse, that your legs are moving but not getting anywhere. It's like those dreams when you are walking without moving, searching for something just out of reach, knowing if you could just take a few more steps everything would be okay. Then you realise you are knee deep in a viscous sludge that wraps around your ankles, then your legs, before pulling tightly around your stomach, the grief centre, probing and coercing, inciting that very special kind of revulsion reserved for the eternally sick and afraid. It all starts in the waking world of childhood exploration, envisioning no end, walking across the land where useless horses are sent to eat grass and die.

Hayley was looking for a horse of which he was particularly fond, a grey Welsh mountain pony called Jack. He had told me that Jack never bit him and liked to nuzzle his shoulder with his nose. Hayley loved to talk of Jack's velvet-soft nose and this was the express purpose of our visit that day. Jack, of course, belonged to the Montereys.

'They've got no kids but they've got a gazillion horses. They don't even look after them properly. Did you see that pink house across the road from the Garage? That's them.' I had. My family had driven past it many times. Affixed to the Monterey's front gate was a large cross made of nine horseshoes or rather, pony shoes, welded together to look like some sort of Christian relic.

'That's the most revolting piece of kitsch I've ever seen in my life,' Father Robert had said. I couldn't tell if he was referring to the cross or the garden gnome in riding garb that stood beside the gate, winking suggestively at passers-by.

'It's a pretty ugly place,' I said as we made our way up the hill.

'Well Mum says it's nice inside,' Hayley said, slightly defensive.

'Your mum is friends with the guy that wants to shoot Agnes?'

'He's not really going to shoot her, I already said that.' He charged ahead of me. Pulling up long blades of grass as he went. Agnes followed.

We were silent for a while and I couldn't bear it so I just said the first thing I could think of.

'Your mum looks like a vampire. She has black eyes and black hair and she hates me.'

'No she doesn't. She's *sick*,' Hayley said in a low tone, picking up a long stick and pounding it into the ground, making a small hole with every step.

'But why was she angry with me?'

'She wasn't angry, she just…can't be awake for very long. She tries but she gets tired. The medicine she takes makes everything blurry. Like when you roll down a hill really fast and then everything starts spinning and you want to puke.'

Hayley stopped to poke a dry, green cow pat with his stick and flicked a round piece off the top. I imagined this would one day happen to Helen's nipples that I had seen, dark and erect under her juvenile nightdress. One day they would just dry up and fall off; thick black hairs would grow from them, so long they could reach out and strangle someone. I couldn't shake the idea that Helen Durston's whole body was slowly crumbling. I went on asking Hayley a lot of stupid questions like if Helen slept a lot during the day, did she have a sleeping sickness? Could she die?

Hayley told me to stop saying stupid shit. He told me to go home. He started to run.

The sky was darkening at a startling pace. Hayley was getting further away from me and started calling for Jack, waving a bouquet of long grass in the air like a desperate offering to an absent god. I looked up at the clouds and a fat droplet of water fell into my eye. It was like weeping in reverse. As the rain got heavier I opened my mouth and drank it, feeling the increasing heaviness on my tongue. It was as though for a minute I became uninhibited — where before I had been so desperate to match Hayley's every step, for a brief moment I was outside of my small, breathless body. It was as though it needed a moment to re-arrange, to attempt to armour my mind from images it would never comprehend. It was like some incorporeal presence was trying to spontaneously fix me, attempting to make me feel indestructible — and it succeeded — but only for a moment before giving up, leaving me facing something terrible. Hayley kneeling; Agnes sniffing at an unidentifiable heap in the long grass. I thought again of that magazine headline. *Chop off my legs.* I ran to them, stopping only when my knees lightly grazed Hayley's back where he sat crying over the decomposing body of a horse. I began asking more questions: What was it? What ate it? Who owns it? He ignored me until I prodded his shoulder and demanded:

'Tell me, is this Jack? Is it Jack? It's not Jack, is it?'

'No. I don't know which one it is. Well, I think I do but I don't know her name. She didn't like people very much. I never petted her or anything. She's a Monterey horse. All the horses are Monterey horses, we're not even allowed here. Go home.'

I looked at the horse, what was left of her, through squinted eyelids in a futile attempt to make the image more palatable. Her ribcage was protruding; long weeds weaving their way up through it. There was enough brown fur still present on the neck and head to give me an idea of what she might have looked like when alive but still the skull, the empty void of the eye socket, rendered the animal nameless. Agnes was nibbling on one of the small pieces of remaining flesh.

Hayley stood up, knocking me aside.

'Bout a week dead,' he said —attempting to spit casually over his shoulder like the cowboys do in the films —but it just ran down his chin in a long dribble. He looked exactly like what he was trying explicitly, in that moment, not to be: a crying child. It was as though someone, something, the same entity that had tried to fix me, had tried to comfort Hayley and given up on him too, because just as soon as he tried to play cowboy his knees buckled and he was on the ground again, sobbing even harder than before.

I asked him to stop. I tugged at his t-shirt. There was a loud clap of thunder nearby. I told him we needed to go back straight away, that I felt sick, that I was scared. Hayley kept telling me no, to shut up, that he had to think, that he had to fix the horse. I sat down behind him and buried my face in the back of his head. His wet hair smelled of cut grass, of petrol.

'I know your mum's not a vampire,' I breathed every syllable into his hair. He turned. His face was bright red and what looked like a small rash had spread below his chin. The bottom half of his face was smeared with snot, tears and dirt. I tried to tidy him up by drawing circles on his cheeks with my finger but it was like when an insect has died on the windscreen of your car and you're low on water for your wipers. The mess just gets re-arranged. It only makes things worse.

Hayley narrowed his eyes.

'Go home now or I'll shoot you.'

I ran, slipping multiple times in the wet grass, only daring to breathe when I stumbled through the front door of my house. My parents believed me when I told them I'd been in the backyard the whole time. They knew I liked to play in the rain.

7 / THE MARE

Whenever Mother Ann drove me past Durston's Garage, I would sink down in my seat. I didn't want Hayley to see me and I didn't want to see him, or Helen, or the Monterey house and its ugly façade. We never patronised Durston's Garage. Mother Ann preferred to fill up the car at the larger garage in town because she'd 'heard things' about Bill Durston and besides, his opening hours were erratic. Bill was known to keep the place locked up for sometimes weeks on end. A high chicken wire fence surrounded two antiquated petrol bowsers and a small kiosk made of concrete blocks.

'You'd think it was a prison,' Mother Ann said when she saw the coils of barbed wire at the top of the fence.

I liked to sit in the backseat of the car, even if there was no one in the front. Mother Ann complained about feeling like a cab driver, but I insisted. Sitting in the front meant I could see the road ahead — and it terrified me. The continual forward motion. I imagined myself flying through the glass and would check every few minutes to see if my seat belt was fastened properly. I decided I preferred the back, the scenery running alongside like a toy I had that moved the scene of a story on with the turn of a handle. It felt like the world was staying beside me rather than forcing me into the future.

I was slumped in the backseat and heard Mother Ann chuckle. Next to me, Louis moaned:

'Mum, Mum, what are you laughing at? Muuuum.'

I leant over, slapped him across the head and told him to shut up. Louis started wailing and reached over to slap me back but his seatbelt held him. Mother Ann reprimanded me, asked me why I had to constantly antagonise my brother, why I had to make everything worse. Louis continued to cry as we parked the car under the house and Mother Ann carried him inside, patting him softly on the back. I sat there in a confused daze, a kind of nervous fugue. I was exhausted. After a while Mother Ann returned and began shaking me gently feeling my forehead in that motherly instinct, happened-on-the-telly way. She took me by the hand and led me upstairs. I went and immediately collapsed onto my bed. Mother Ann suggested I have a nap. I buried myself under the covers and asked her what she was laughing at before I hit Louis.

'A silly thing, really,' she said. 'I just saw that the Montereys had taken that horseshoe cross your father hates off the front of their gate.'

What was it even for? I wondered. Was it the only horseshoe cross in existence? Did it encourage five generations of pedigree thoroughbreds and ward off creatures of the night? Hayley must have stolen it. To send a message that they shouldn't leave their failed show ponies out in a field to die. I rolled over onto my stomach and Mother Ann patted my back gently.

'This is how I used to get you to sleep when you were a baby,' I heard her say.

What followed was disordered half-slumber. I could still hear my parents talking in the other room, Louis grunting and squealing in front of the television. I saw irregular shapes moving around, like when you close your eyes in direct sunlight and you see shades of black and orange and yellow flicker around. An erratic kaleidoscope. I could smell the musk sticks Mother Ann would buy for me after swimming lessons at the local pool near our old house. I could almost taste them.

For the briefest moment I felt safe, but the sweetness in my mouth turned sour and the dancing shadows turned dark, pooling together to form the outline of a person. It was a black void. No distinct characteristics, but I knew it was a man. I started calling for Mother Ann. I had no idea if she could hear me. The call became a scream. I felt like I had been screaming for hours, I felt hoarse, I couldn't wake up no matter how hard I tried but eventually my mother was by my side, shaking me awake.

Louis flew into the room and rolled on top of me asking over and over again why I was sleeping. I pushed him off and he started lazily kicking the wall and humming to himself.

I reached for Mother Ann.

'I was calling for ages. Didn't you hear me, where were you?'

'I was right outside. I came as soon as I heard you.'

'But it felt like…'

'You don't sleep durin' the daaay,' said Louis in an odd exaggerated drawl.

I had to tense every muscle in my body to stop myself lashing out at him again. His voice was deafening and he never shut up and I could never make myself heard over the stupid repetitive bullshit he seemed to expel when I needed my mother the most.

'Do you know who Mister San Hosantio is?' I asked Mother Ann.

Louis had begun to kick the wall far too hard and she could only manage a half-hearted 'No idea, honey,' before dragging my brother out of the room.

'San Santy-oh!' said Louis as Mother Ann closed the door behind them.

I don't know where I first heard the name Mister San Hosantio. Couldn't recall hearing anyone speak in the dream, I just woke up with a desperate urge to say this name. I've heard a lot of stories about people who feel a shadow haunting them in their peripheries, something awful in the sidelines and you know that if you turn your head only slightly you would see something too horrible to bear. So, you never look. You train yourself to never look but you are left with the feeling that it's walking right in front of you, it's standing too close behind you in a queue, it's deliberately nudging you with a trolley at the supermarket, it's every car that follows you for so long it can't possibly be a coincidence. It's the grown men that pass you in the street when you're barely twelve years old and make guttural, animal sounds. Every grandfather that feels the need to comment on how much you're 'developing' before patting you on the arse.

8 / GODDESS OF DOORS

The same day the cross disappeared from the Monterey's front gate, the same day I dreamed of Mister San Hosantio for the first time, my dream cottage – my empty, haunted, colonial vessel with the bay windows – was taken from me. I was in such a stupor over the cross that as we pulled into our driveway that afternoon I didn't notice the 'sold' sticker plastered over Jan Boynahan's sign.

'Maybe one day when you're grown up you will have a place just like it. When you're rich and famous.' Mother Ann widened her eyes at me from across the dinner table, as if trying to imbue me with some kind of quaint optimism. Father Robert scoffed into his lentils. He is a vegetarian. One of Mother Ann's many ridiculous jobs was making three separate meals every night. 'Lucky we like the same stuff, hey Al?' she once said, gently scratching my back the way I liked. 'Thank god for you.'

Father Robert's scoff is the sound I always hear when I doubt myself. I would never own a house. I didn't – still don't – trust myself to own anything. You must work to own things. You must want to join in on life. He told Mother Ann to stop giving me false hope, while Louis sat rubbing miso paste into the table. All Louis ate was miso paste spread onto dry, wheat-free crackers. He thought it was Vegemite, but he couldn't eat that. It made his stomach ache resulting in a colic attack. We had to perform many covert operations like this to avoid a meltdown. The smell of the miso was overpowering. Louis' stomach problems seemed like an excuse my parents made up. Because they couldn't properly understand what was going on in his mind, they chose to focus on something physical, to give his pain legitimacy.

I went to bed straight after dinner. I heard my parents arguing in their room. Father Robert's mumbles were always too low to hear but I could get the gist of the conversation from my mother's loud exasperated responses about him 'doing bugger all' and his 'negative attitude'.

A week later, Father Robert Howard had moved out. He went back to the city to live in a run-down, two-bedroom unit owned by his parents. To a place where he could ignore even the most well-intentioned solicitations, in peace. Mother Ann kept his name. She couldn't explain why, aside from the fact that they were only separated and remain so to this day. In a fit of rage, I demanded I change my name, not to Mother Ann's maiden name, Byrne, but to something else entirely. One day I declared I wanted no surname at all, that I wanted to be known merely as 'Jennifer'. All the prettiest girls in American movies were called Jennifer. Mother Ann firmly instructed me to keep the name Alberta Howard until I was eighteen and old enough to make up my own mind. She said by then I would think the idea of being Jennifer silly and besides, I might be thinking about marriage myself by then. I might meet my future husband in high school like she did. I said: 'but your marriage didn't work,' and she ran off – I assumed – to cry. I never saw any of the adults around me cry. At school it was discouraged. Crying was a shameful, weak activity that, if you absolutely must, should be engaged in privately. I thought that maybe that was why Hayley threatened to shoot me, because I might tell people I saw him cry.

My maternal grandparents had always planned on moving closer to us and my parents' separation only accelerated their plans. Ma and Pa bought a small brick house with a tidy garden in a new estate a few streets away from us. A dairy farmer had sold and sub-divided his land and it was now full of dull, identical bungalows that seemed out of place in the rural landscape. I wondered about the remains of dead livestock that were likely buried underneath the house, whether Ma and Pa would be haunted by a devil pony or a starving ewe that sings like a human child or the ghost of a little boy who once tried to transform himself into a beast.

I rarely saw Hayley at school. When we did spot each other across the playground we would both run in the opposite direction. That stopped me from believing he really wanted to hurt me, but whenever I played outside I stayed away from the road, just in case he cycled by. I missed Agnes though.

'Weird time to be doing it, but whatever works for them, I suppose.'

Mother Ann had come into my room on a Thursday afternoon to tell me people had started moving into the house across the road. My house. After ploughing through my reading comprehension homework, I made my way warily up to the fence and hid amongst the bushes that lined the front fence. I saw some removalists grappling with a white leather sofa; a blond man in very neat clothing giving them stern orders. I watched him carry a few small boxes inside, stopping frequently to roll up his shirt sleeves that wouldn't seem to stay put above his elbows.

A girl emerged from the house, holding a white Persian cat around its middle, swinging its legs from side to side; a disgruntled head lay otherwise compliant against her chest. She was humming a high-pitched, improvised lullaby to the feline, shushing it when it dared voice its discomfort. I thought it would be the worst time for Hayley to show up – the worst time for him to come pedalling down the street and inevitably introduce himself to this girl the same way he had with me but with more enthusiasm, because even though this girl looked quite a lot like me, she looked somehow superior (I would assume anyone that was able to live in that house superior). Besides, who knew how many 'friends' he'd accumulated peddling around town like a tiny, amiable vagrant? She didn't look like she would like to be friends with him. Or me, for that matter. I wanted to talk to her. Mother Ann kept saying I needed a 'proper female friend', but I didn't know how to be a 'proper' child. I couldn't boldly present myself like Hayley could. She looked like the version of myself I imagined I would find in a wax museum. If I were made of wax and they were to give my nose a bit of a pinch, enlarge my ears, arch my eyebrows slightly.

Widen my mouth. But the longer I looked at her I realised the only feature we truly had in common was long, brown hair.

I was certain she couldn't see me, but there was no way I could reveal myself. My increasing heartbeat told me no – toes digging into the cold grass, my shaking calves telling me no. Regardless, my voice hurtled through the shrubbery before I had a chance to stop it.

'I like your cat!'

The girl jumped in an exaggerated manner and glared in my direction.

'Thank you. Are you a talking bush?' She crossed the road and dropped the cat by the fence.

I crouched down and tried to crawl silently towards a dense clump of privet, where I would be less exposed but still clock any movement on the other side.

'Find the person, Janus. I command you. Maybe, if they like you, you can live with them, you bum hole.' Janus purred with annoyance and walked back towards the house. The girl ignored her and began pouring through the privet, tearing at foliage, gripping the wire fence with her fingers and shaking it, making exasperated groans. 'Come out.'

If I were to make a run for it she would see me. I sat waiting for the inevitable. She fed a twig through the wire that failed to reach my shoulder and it fell silently by my side. I stood with some consolation in the fact she could still not see me from the nose down.

'Oh hi!' she sounded out of breath. 'Do you want to come out and meet my cat? I'll get her back, hang on a sec – Janus! Stupid cat!' The blond man I assumed was her father tried to call her back, telling her to stop making a scene.

'Yeah, steady on love,' said a bulky removalist with several tattoos.

'Steady on yourself, wanker!' the girl replied.

'Laura!' her father shouted. 'Inside. Now.'

'But I found a person in the bushes.'

Laura's father didn't bother pressing the matter. I noticed he had quite a pleasant face. Not as tired as my father. Not as bearded. Younger – but more experienced. I could tell he was the kind of person who had lived yet kept all the sordid details to himself.

'Well, Uncle Mel will be here any minute so make sure you say hello.' He fiddled again with his shirt sleeves and returned to not helping unpack the truck. He didn't seem to care about anything. His daughter seemed, to him, a triviality. I would never have gotten away with swearing at a removalist and refusing to do as I was told in the space of a few seconds.

Laura moved closer and lowered her voice.

'These moving men are really yuck. One has a tattoo of some naked boobs. Can you please talk to me? I mean you're acting like you don't want to and your eyes are going everywhere so I can't tell where you're looking but that's okay, there's been lots of...' she took a deep breath, '...weird stuff happening.' Her tone was suddenly vulnerable. 'Please?' she asked, plucking more leaves from the bush as though such a minor task could uncover me completely. She pointed toward the gate and coerced me to come out onto the footpath. She said if I did so, Janus the cat might come back and let me pet her. I did as she asked, moving quickly, almost at a run, all the nervous adrenalin in my system forcing me to perform every task in a reckless manner while my brain said no, danger, fear her. Amidst such turmoil I unlatched the heavy steel gate and swung it aside.

'Big gate. You got cows or something? Are you a farm? Everyone here is a farm.'

I wasn't sure if a person could 'be' a farm. I shook my head.

'The gate came with the house. But I might be getting a dog soon so...'

Her eyes lit up. 'You like cats and dogs?'

I nodded. 'I like all animals. Except cane toads. Do you like them?'

'Nah, yuck,' said Laura.

'I'm so glad. Did you know they can throw their guts up and pretend to be dead and then suck it all back in and carry on living?'

'People do that too. I mean they don't puke their actual guts out, but I've made myself puke before. You put pepper and vinegar in some water and drink it fast. I got a day off school once when I did that. But yeah, toads are gross but it's great you love most animals, I think everyone should — I mean, I love Janus even though she's a bum-hole shit — sometimes she lets me cuddle her.'

I giggled. I liked her inventive swears, her scatological humour. She squealed with delight when she found out we were the same age. She was wearing a white sweatshirt covered in pastel clouds. Across the chest, two childlike angels embraced each other on a cloud surrounded by text that read 'Little Twin Stars'. I took a closer look at her hair. It was very much like mine. Perhaps a little longer, reaching the lowest point of her back. It was unkempt, looked like it matted easily like mine — thick and couldn't decide if it was wavy or straight. It wasn't exactly like looking in a mirror. I had a small pouting mouth that turned down a little at the sides, making me look perpetually sad. Laura's mouth was wider and filled her whole face when she grinned. My eyes were wide and far apart, Laura's were deep set, with dark pigment around them that looked like bruises or smudged eyeliner. Sometimes when she was tired or upset she looked like she had two black eyes.

It was as though my meeting with Hayley was replaying itself but this time the tightness that gripped my body wasn't half as intense.

'So, you are Laura?' I asked, staring at my feet as I realised I had been inspecting her too hard. I may have even looked her in the eye. Just briefly, just for a second. Maybe.

'Yes! I am Laura Clemence. You're supposed to say it Clo-mons but most people say Clem-ens. It's French. We're French.'

'You don't sound very French.'

'Um, Daddy's been to France. For work. His mother is French but he was born in England then moved here when he was ten. My Grand-maman is going to teach me some French words.'

Laura went on to tell me, with no coercion on my part, that she barely remembered her mother, that she had left her father before Laura's first birthday. All she seemed to have left of her mother was her best friend, Valerie.

'She's our housekeeper, now, is Valerie. I said she was my mum's best friend, but of course they aren't anymore because when Mum ran away from us Val stayed — said she was on our side. Daddy tells me I should always be nice to Val because even though she's weird, she is loyal. She'll be living in the flat out the back. Do you still have two parents?'

I shook my head. 'They split up. It's just me and Mother Ann — my mum — and my brother.'

'I'm an only child,' said Laura. 'It's boring.'

I didn't want to tell her too much about Louis. I said it was boring having a brother, too. Laura gasped, then, realising she hadn't asked my name, she looked at me expectantly, like she was hoping it would be something like Celeste Moreau or Jeanne Chevalier.

'Alberta. Alberta Howard.'

'Albert then? Is that the girl version of Albert?'

'Yeah, but my mum calls me Al, and my friend Hayley — we used to be friends — he called me Albert. He liked to call me Albert because it's a boy's name and Hayley is a girl's name.

Laura asked me why Hayley and I weren't friends anymore as she fell clumsily into a sitting position on the grass. I joined her, crossing my legs underneath me tightly, gripping my knees. I said Hayley said he would shoot me, but he was really upset at the time and that it didn't really matter because I'd heard that girls and boys weren't supposed to be friends.

Laura blew a dismissive raspberry as a rumbling blue panel van pulled up next to us.

'Oh no, it's Uncle Melvin. He pretends to be an actor but he's not. He also runs a health food shop — it's terrible, it's tiny and it stinks of carob and sprouts. He'll never be famous. He's been living in this town for years and years.'

A man who looked like Laura's father, but with a rounder face and hair that looked like it had been poorly bleached, stumbled out of the driver's seat. He was wearing flared jeans. 'Oi oi love!' he called over to Laura in a cockney accent.

'Hullo Uncle Mel,' said Laura, unenthused.

'Aw, chin up. Got a little mate already?' I wondered how he even had time to register my presence as he was already halfway indoors. We could hear him shouting greetings to his brother inside.

'He thinks he's Oliver Reed,' said Laura with a sigh.

'I don't know who that is,' I said.

Laura nodded.

'I don't know either. That's just what Daddy says when Uncle Mel drinks. Val says I don't need to know who Oliver Reed is because she saw him once in a film when he wrestles a man and you can see their willies flying about. Anyway, when Uncle Mel is being Oliver Reed it means he's being a right drunk bastard. Old soak, Val says. But Uncle Mel thinks he looks like some German…I forget his name.'

We sat there for ages, Laura telling me in hushed tones about the removalists, how they had, before I arrived, scratched the polished mahogany floor by dragging her father's bookcase into his study instead of carrying it and, rather than confront them about it, her father pulled the collar of his shirt up over his nose and starting breathing hard and fast. Laura said she'd never seen him do something so odd in her life.

'He's usually really cranky when things like that happen,' she said, 'I thought he was going to yell at them but he — I think he was scared they'd beat him up or something. I mean, they could, couldn't they?'

Janus finally sauntered over to us and let me stroke her a little. Then as the removalists were preparing to leave they started laughing. Laura had her back to them and I whispered to her, startled, that I thought they were laughing — staring — at us. Laura jumped to her feet, turned to them and screamed:

'What? What are you staring at? What?'

'Call me when you're older!' the younger of the two barked out the window as he started the engine. As they drove away they honked the horn. Laura stood staring as the truck rounded the corner. Once it was out of sight, she took an uneven breath out. She noticed my unease.

'Don't worry about it. They're going back where they belong. To Garbage City.' She grinned at me again and the sickness subsided.

'My dad went back to Garbage City.'

Laura nodded. 'He drive a truck? They all do.'

With Laura, I didn't feel nervous like I did around Hayley. We had conversations. Most of the time I had spent with Hayley had been in silence as though he was just desperate for a shadow, someone to follow him. But with Laura, I could tell her things and she would understand. She only had one parent, she was able to say things that I found difficult to say. I had found a shield.

9 / NEW HOLLYWOOD

Everything opened. Our house opened — to Mother Ann's work friends, my aunt Julia, who visited one night and the two of them drank and badmouthed Father Robert. Louis had left a pellet of dry turd in my bed, but I didn't tell Mother Ann, not while Aunt Julia was staying. She was enjoying speaking and being (somewhat) listened to and having another adult speak back in a language she could understand. Aunt Julia was a school teacher and her husband was head of a popular chain of furniture stores. They had one daughter, Bethany, who was a few years older than me and already tipped to be a professional athlete. She was a runner. Mother Ann changed the way she spoke around her sister. She became more critical of people (her accent developed more of a lower-class inflection, the kind Father Robert hated) she spoke of everything in a more superficial manner, but most of the time she would catch herself doing it and attempt to rectify it with criticisms of Julia's parenting, or praise the way Louis made little intricate sculptures out of Blu-tac, leaving out the part where he rubbed them into the carpet after showing them to her, or the time when I lay on the couch and ended up with a big wad of it in my hair and I had to chop it out with scissors, leaving a short tuft of hair sticking out of the back of my head.

Lying in bed, I heard them comparing Bethany and me.

'I don't think she'll be particularly sporty,' Mother Ann said. 'She's active around her friend across the road but they seem so obsessed with films. All they want to do of a weekend is rent videos.'

'I don't think she'd enjoy athletics,' said Aunt Julia.

'Might do her good though,' said Mother Ann. 'She's got thick legs already. Robert's mother doesn't have ankles, she gets it from his side. Blames it on her water retention or rheumatoid arthritis or whatever illness she decides to have that week.'

'Al's probably just copying your eating habits,' Aunt Julia laughed. I wanted to get out of bed and choke her. 'Bethany is doing so well. Her skin's looking great. Got her a Clinique subscription.'

'Julia, she's eleven years old.' Mother Ann sighed and I heard the glug glug of a glass of wine being re-filled.

They went on with this hideous conversation well into the night and I lay there, every muscle tense, my teeth clenched waiting for another mention of my name, wondering when Mother Ann would realise she was being a hypocrite for speaking of me the same way Aunt Julia spoke of her, as though it earned her extra Julia points to belittle her daughter. After a while, the topic changed from the appropriate age to let a girl get her ears pierced to Bethany's thriving social life. Apparently, Bethany had thirty-five kids show up to her birthday party. She had a cake from *The Women's Weekly Children's Birthday Cake Book*, that was fashioned to look like a swimming pool by sticking chocolate finger biscuits around the edge of a rectangular sponge cake and topping it off with green jelly to look like water. Aunt Julia said she loved baking but it made it so hard for her to stick to the Pritikin diet. She laughed for far too long about that. Mother Ann told her I didn't really have a party for my ninth birthday, that I didn't even express the desire for one, that I was happy with her taking Laura and me to the movies.

Then, she lowered her voice, as if part of her knew I was listening. I quietly stepped out of bed and placed my ear against the door. I heard Mother Ann say something about being glad I'm not 'hanging around the boy up the road any more the one with...' I didn't get to hear what Hayley had because Aunt Julia started loudly inquiring what the deal was with 'the divorcee across the road'. Mother Ann shushed her and said something like she had no idea, that she'd only spoken to Jonathan a few times, that in those times he never thanked her for driving 'that ratbag' Laura about when nobody else could. Then, her voice elevated as though she was so annoyed by Jonathan Clemence that she'd relieved herself of any indiscretion:

'He always has this look on his face like he's just stepped in dog poo. Smokes like a bloody chimney. Lit up in front of me the other day and virtually blew it in my face.'

Aunt Julia scoffed.

'And you let Alberta go over there so often? Well, most of Beth's friend's mothers are on the P and C or the Little Athletics committee so I don't have to worry. Good homes.'

'Plenty of money,' Mother Ann added.

'Well, we're comfortable,' said Aunt Julia.

In the morning, I asked Mother Ann what other parts of my body she thought were 'thick'. She told me she wasn't sure what I was talking about. Aunt Julia sat at the kitchen table in a pink bathrobe and I am sure I saw her smirk as she brought her coffee cup to her lips.

With Father Robert gone, I knew I was allowed to have friends over, but still, I couldn't do it. Especially after finding out how much Mother Ann disliked Laura. But I still blamed Father Robert the most. He ruined it all by giving me that sickness, the sickness that made me think Laura would be disgusted by Louis — his noises, his pica, his need for openly onanistic behaviours, by our wicker couch with the yellow, half-eaten foam cushions. Mother Ann constantly said she wanted to find the time to sew new cushion covers but didn't want to invest the time and money only to have Louis ruin them. He'd recently kicked a hole into the bathroom wall. I couldn't let Laura into that place. It was the toad's fault, the headless nun's fault. It was Mister San Hosantio's fault. Someone or something had done something to make life difficult for us, that's all I could gather.

I coveted the Clemence house. In Laura's room, I could look out of those bay windows instead of in. I would lay my head on her bed and watch her fiddling with a tiny yellow tape deck, playing her collection of cassettes and showing me a dance she had choreographed to Top 40 songs she had recorded off the radio. When there was no such thing as a guilty pleasure and you could emancipate yourself in the comfort of your own bedroom.

I asked Laura if her father was rich. She shrugged. I still don't know what Jonathan Clemence's occupation was. He had a 'government job' — that was it. There was some mention of being an advisor for an MP in a nearby electorate. But you don't push the issue regarding someone's occupation when you are young. You don't care where people get their money from. When you grow up with a lot of it, I suspect you would never question its origins. Even in my family, running solely on my mother's low wages, the single mothers and carer's pension, she always pulled enough together to get by without me noticing and 'having to worry' as she had put it later. She borrowed a lot from her parents, but I didn't feel like we were that underprivileged. Not compared to the Durstons. But then I saw the interior of Laura's house, with all the space-age gadgetry and couches that were not for sitting on and I never wanted to go home.

Laura said that Daddy Jonathan (she had decided to emulate my style of parental nomenclature) made the decision to move to the country because he thought it would be a better place for her to grow up and even though he was always travelling for work, he had Valerie and his brother Melvin to look out for her. Valerie was short, with a very similar body to Mother Ann — round and soft. She was an eccentric dresser, in her early forties, staunchly opinionated and educated (she would often correct Melvin on film trivia) but superstitious, or at least that's what I thought it was. She couldn't bear to look at Laura. She never looked her in the eye when speaking to her, sometimes even physically placing her hand over the side of her face lest she catch a disease, a Laura curse. Even so, she managed to perform basic parenting duties, whether Jonathan was home or not.

I could always sense that Laura was tired of being called 'capable'. The assumption that she could survive parental neglect because she was 'effervescent', as her end of year report card had read.

'Effervescent schmeffervescent,' Laura said under her breath after her family praised her for settling into her new school so well.

We were all sitting in the Clemence lounge room, the adults on the plush white leather sofas, Laura and I on the floor.

'That was a very nice thing for your teacher to say; you should be proud,' Valerie said to a large, slightly faded print of John William Waterhouse's 'The Lady of Shalott' behind Laura's head ('This is our only art,' Laura had announced with fervour on my first visit).

Daddy Jonathan tapped some ash from his cigarette into an empty wine glass.

'It's always best to be jolly,' Uncle Melvin had said to no one in particular, swirling a glass of red wine and shuffling in barefoot on the cream shag pile carpet to 'Rasputin' by Boney M.

'Who is he today?' I asked Laura.

Laura tossed the report card over her shoulder and studied her uncle for a moment, hands on hips. 'I don't know. Who are you today, Uncle Mel?'

'Rasputin,' Valerie said, in a monotone, unamused voice as the song faded out.

'Is he the German you think Mel looks like?' Laura asked.

'That's Klaus Kinski,' Daddy Jonathan said, rubbing his temple with his cigarette-free hand as though we were all giving him a dreadful headache.

'He's a bloody creep, that man,' Valerie shuddered.

Melvin was busy concentrating on changing the record with one hand while taking a sip of red wine with the other. 'You're So Vain' by Carly Simon began. Uncle Melvin motioned for us to come and dance with him.

'No, Uncle Mel,' said Laura, 'I told you, I don't dance with people.'

'What do you call those dance classes your father pays for then?' Valerie asked.

'That's professional. If you're just moving around your lounge room like a big nerd it's just really, really embarrassing.'

Melvin attempted a flamboyant twirl in order to further provoke his niece and ended up spilling wine all over the carpet. He yelped and ran to the kitchen. Jonathan and Valerie just sat there, staring at the Lady of Shallot.

Laura told me, 'Mel and Daddy Jonathan like Carly Simon, because

on the cover of the record, you can see her boobs through her top.'
Instinctively, I crossed my arms over my chest.

'Like Linda Ronstadt,' I said.

Melvin overheard as he rushed back in and started dabbing at the
carpet with a wet sponge.

'Oh, no. Those country ladies are all so *needy*.'

The more I saw of Melvin Clemence, the less fazed I was by his
behaviour. I knew Mother Ann would call him a 'ratbag'. I became less
fearful of his drunken slurs, most of which went over our head but
sometimes Laura would translate for me, usually when he was referring to an ex. 'He's talking about Sandra, they broke up when I was a
baby, she did the dirty on him.' It was as though he forgot we were in
the room half the time. This talk didn't make me sick, like that day
with the removalists. Melvin seemed to belong in an anachronistic
bawdy nineteen seventies adult fantasy world that could not entirely
harm us. Or maybe I just trusted him because Laura did.

I liked being bored back then. It was a comforting boredom. Nowadays, every thought that enters my mind is a new death and I expect
these deaths will multiply the older I get. Children experience tedium
in a different manner — any claims of boredom and passing whims
were easily remedied by the power of suggestion, or the presence of
company. The delightful mundanity of lying on Laura's bed, watching
her crochet. She said her grandmaman had taught her, but it was
Valerie who had put in most of the hours.

'Val likes ugly, pale colours,' Laura told me. Laura liked bright
colours with black — electric blue with black, neon yellow with black.
She twisted the needles in and out musing:

'One day I'm going to paint my room black. Probably when I'm a
teenager.'

I lay watching her complete a square of dark purple (at my
request). When she was done, she tossed it to me and said, 'There. No
More crotch-it today, I couldn't be bothered. Merry early Christmas.'
Children cope with boredom, but no one said they possessed patience.

'Pretty,' I said, turning it over in my hands. 'What should I use it
for?'

'Doily? Stinky old woman doily? You can put your cups of tea
down on it and never wash the stains off it and when you are living at

the smelly old person's home it will smell like mothballs but you will keep it forever because you couldn't bear to throw out such a precious hair-loom.'

'What if you're at the smelly old person's home with me?' I asked her.

Laura thought for a moment.

'If we became old together we'd be in the looney bin, in the old person section for old ladies that aren't married.'

'And wee their pants,' I added.

'Yeah and Uncle Mel's bonkers ex-girlfriends will be there and my mum probably.'

Hayley's mum too, I thought.

'We could both have dead husbands?' I suggested.

'That won't get you in the looney bin. The husbands put their wives in there to make them disappear so they can screw other ladies.' Laura sighed as though a weight she wasn't ready for had suddenly descended upon her.

10 / REPROBATE

At Christmas, Daddy Jonathan took Laura to the city for a few weeks to see her grandmaman (Grandpapa was in the war and died 'not in the war but because of the war,' Laura said), and an army of cousins she barely knew. I stayed at home, but Mother Ann cooked an elaborate Christmas lunch, as usual.

'Champagne on a beer budget,' I heard Ma whisper to Pa before they all but licked their plates clean. Ma was a cold and objective woman, like an even more conservative version of Julia, with a tornado of permed strawberry blonde hair on top of her head. Pa had no hair at all (by choice, because it was 'easier') and could be described as jovial; others seemed to see him as an amiable person, a gentle person. Mother Ann said Father Robert was belted over the backside all the time as a child. Pa would never. Pa would catch spiders and let them free in the garden. Pa would never.

Mother Ann often overcompensated with cooking. This particular Christmas, she cooked away her guilt at being a single mother that relied too heavily on her parents. She tried her best to please them, to repay them in any way she could. Aunt Julia, Uncle Lyle and Bethany were also there. Bethany was bemoaning the fact that she couldn't go join her parents on their recent trip to Paris.

'But I bought you a beret you never wear, and that lovely Jacadi coat,' said Aunt Julia.

'It's always too hot to wear those things around here,' said Bethany.

'My friend is part French,' I said. Everyone ignored me, instead choosing to remind Bethany of all the lovely Christmas presents she'd got.

Mother Ann leaned over and whispered in my ear:

'They don't even remember walking through the Louvre, they just know they did it.'

She and Father Robert had gone for a trip in a campervan around Europe for their honeymoon and whenever Mother Ann felt down about not having as much money as her sister, she would talk about how she wanted to go back there and how she didn't understand why Aunt Julia and Uncle Lyle bothered spending so much money just to recklessly charge through cultural capitals on a drunken Contiki Tour.

Louis was splashing around naked in an inflatable paddling pool screeching at the top of his lungs about Thomas the Tank Engine, surrounded by the floating remains of paper hats from Christmas crackers and a large rubber duck he had received from Aunt Julia and Uncle Lyle, who on arrival had handed the gift to me with the instruction to 'give that to your brother' so they didn't have to engage with him. I was hyperactive due to copious quantities of rich tiramisu that I had sneaked when no one was watching. I was also miffed that no one was paying any attention to me.

I sidled up to my aunt and uncle and said, loudly,

'Louis likes his duck!' The adults kept talking amongst themselves. I decided to test a word I heard Laura use while we were jumping on her trampoline. She did a high kick in mid-air and yelled, 'Fuck!'. I didn't know what the word meant but her high kick impressed me. I thought it must be a word you use in gymnastics or karate. I leaped over to Bethany and kicked my leg right at her face.

'Fuck!' I yelled. Proud of myself.

'Ann! What did she just say?' Uncle Lyle shifted in his director's chair, outraged. His hand shook with anger as it clasped tighter around his *It's a Knockout* stubbie holder.

'She tried to kick me,' said Bethany.

'Where did you get that word from young lady?' asked Pa, a mouthful of potato salad.

'It's a word you say in sports. Uncle Lyle did you hear what I said? Louis likes his duck, I said *duck*. I'm trying to tell you Louis likes his

duck. Also —' This time I screamed the word at the top of my lungs, '
— Fuck!'

Uncle Lyle stood up and started clenching his fists like he wanted
to punch me. I surprised myself how bold I had become with the help
of a little bit of caffeine. Uncle Lyle demanded an explanation. I
refused to give him one and ran off to my room, leaving Mother Ann
to give it for me. She was furious. She still fails to understand why I
am so horrible at parties. Last year, I ruined her fiftieth birthday by
drinking an entire half-cask of sauvignon blanc and stumbling about
handing out canapés to our extended family and Mother Ann's work
colleagues. Apparently, I asked her boss what he thought the worst
swear word he had ever heard was and proceeded to rattle off a list of
some of my favourites. I did a sardonic twirl in front of Aunt Julia and
Bethany (who by then was state champion for running in pointless
circles or throwing the shot hammer) asking them to 'go to town', to
tell me what's wrong with my body, at one point offering to get a felt
pen so they could circle all the bits that repulsed them. I remember
Mother Ann pulled me roughly aside and told me she had never been
more ashamed. I started screaming, 'Black sheep! Black sheep!' and
passed out on my bedroom floor. I wanted to do what confident people
did at parties and when I was still anxious after a few drinks I had a
few more, desperate to feel content, to feel ordinary.

11 / WE LOVE BOYZONE

By the time Laura returned we only had a few more weeks of summer holidays to go before school returned. Laura knew about Hayley, but not much. The handful of times we had seen him at school she would stand in front of me so he wouldn't shoot me. She was a little taller than me and it felt safe. I wanted to tell her about the dead horse and the missing cross. I was hoping she could rationalise the entire situation for me. I needed someone to tell me I shouldn't be afraid. She had asked me a lot of questions about Hayley: Why would he want to hang around with a girl, a younger one at that? Did he have any French in him? Was he a 'deep' person? I wasn't sure how to answer that one — I didn't understand what she meant by 'deep'. I said I wasn't sure, his body surely held as much blood and guts as the next child, though he was very short and thin for his age, I supposed. Then there was this:

'Did you pretend Hayley was your brother so you can have a normal brother to play with?'

She hadn't met Louis, but she had heard him. The whole neighbourhood heard him. The whole school heard him. I pretended I didn't know the boy screaming over the Principal at Monday assembly. I had explained Louis to Laura the way I did to Hayley (who obviously had questions the day he knocked on my door), that Louis couldn't communicate the same way she and I could. He would probably act like a four-year-old forever. Sometimes he got very upset about very small things. No one really understood any of it. Laura just shrugged and told me about her cousin Corbin; how she dropped him on his head when he was a baby.

'He didn't fall very hard at all, but I just felt so bad when it happened that I cried for three days. They shouldn't have let me touch him anyway because everything I touch seems to go bad, but now — now they think he might have a damaged brain and even though they say it's not my fault, I think it might be. I don't know because Corbin is my Aunt Lucy's baby, and Daddy Jonathan and Uncle Mel don't like her, so I never see them.'

Even after both Hayley and Laura had expressed a casual acceptance of my brother, I still felt that they would abandon me if they knew too much. If they saw what our couch looked like. If they smelled the bathroom. Saw the holes in the wall. I wondered if Laura's cousin Corbin hit people.

I was spending the night at Laura's because the next day the school would be releasing all the class lists for the coming year and Mother Ann was going to take us to check which class we were in on the school bulletin board then take us shopping for school supplies. Of course, we hoped to be in the same class and decided to spend the night in each other's company as though this closeness would somehow will it so. I was worried about what would happen if we were separated, from the immediate effects — stationery shopping would be tense and likely ruined, I would cry and cry more if Laura wasn't upset as well (I had never seen her cry), to the long-term ones — what if Laura no longer wanted to be my friend? I was trying to find the courage to voice my fears as we watched a Saturday morning sitcom about a boy band that I didn't find particularly amusing. Laura was talking all the way through it about how an older cousin had explained to her about how boy bands are put together so there is a 'type' of boy for every girl.

'But,' she asked, 'what happens if you don't like any of the boys in the band? Does that mean that there are no boys for you anywhere? That you're the wrong kind of girl? Like you're insane and you can't have a boyfriend? Uncle Melvin said his ex-girlfriend was insane because she liked other girls and hated men.'

We stared at the TV. The boy band was singing a song about working out and sweating. I said I didn't mind the one with the floppy hair. Laura said I was predictable.

There was a knock on the door and soon Valerie entered, flustered, saying 'Laura, boy for sale.'

'Huh?' Laura turned around and looked quizzically at Valerie who quickly turned her head and muttered:

'Boy. At the door. For Alberta, small, looks like an orphan, just tell him to bugger off. I don't do chocolate drives or pie drives or donations to the boy scouts, your father doesn't pay me enough for that.' She turned towards the kitchen singing 'Boy for Sale' over and over again in a low melancholy voice.

'It's a song from some musical. I hate musicals,' said Laura, noticing my confusion. She started towards the door but I grabbed her arm.

'Hang on a sec.'

'You say that all the time. Hang on hang on hang on, wait, wait, wait.' She tried to pull away from me but my fingers clutched at her t-shirt, claw-like, desperate, exposing a thin white shoulder with three brown moles in the shape of a triangle. Sometimes I liked to connect the dots with a felt pen and pretend I was giving Laura a tattoo. 'He's probably come to say sorry for wanting to kill you and stuff.'

'I — I don't know…could you tell him to go away? I don't think I can. We haven't talked for so long and some bad stuff happened that I can't tell you about. He's just going to be annoying anyway — I mean, not in the way Valerie thinks, like, Hayley would never be in scouts — he just asks a lot of questions.'

I then realised that the only way Hayley would know I was at Laura's house was if he'd gone to my house first. I was now grappling with the additional anxiety of Mother Ann being angry with me. She seemed to know something bad about the Durstons that I didn't.

Laura told me that if Mother Ann had a problem with me speaking to Hayley then she wouldn't have told him where I was. She gently prised my fingers from her t-shirt.

'Well, why don't you hide and I'll tell him you're sick or something?'

The idea of hiding was tempting, but I didn't like the idea of not being present when Laura and Hayley met. They might conspire against me.

'All right,' I said, 'but I'll have to block my ears, too.' What I couldn't hear couldn't hurt me.

Laura screwed her face up.

'Um, why?'

'I get embarrassed listening to people talk. I don't know why, but I hate listening to Mother Ann make phone calls and stuff.' In truth, this had started when one day I tried to answer the phone myself and a low female voice on the end of the line whispered: 'Mr Howard, I love you,' and promptly hung up. I told Mother Ann and she explained that it was just some prank callers, bored teenagers who had found our number at random in the White Pages. But that couldn't be it. Maybe there was a woman that did love my father? A dead woman, a headless woman? More than that, I felt humiliated. Just as I was making the smallest attempt at independence. Whenever I tried something new, to master a task as mundane as making a phone call, it felt like the world was going to burn up, or the sun would explode and kill us all which was fine with me, anything to avoid making a phone call. I thought for a minute about how I could explain this to Laura.

"You know, it's like you were saying about how you hate hearing other people go to the toilet? How at school you like to go when the toilet block is empty cause —'

Laura made a gagging sound.

'I get it, I get it. Okay, hide behind the couch, block your ears, I'll go quick.'

I ducked behind the sofa. I lay on my stomach against the cream shag pile carpet and dug my fingers into my ears as far as they could go, until my fingernails dug into my ear canal, the slight pain a welcome distraction. I'd thrown Laura out like a socially adept grenade. Soon, I could hear the distant hum of voices. Laura's mostly. Neither of us knew the meaning of what adults called an 'inside voice'. I tried to imagine what they were saying to each other:

Laura: *Hello I am Laura.*
Hayley: *Hello I am Hayley.*
Laura: *Do you like to work out?*

Hayley: *Not really…*

Laura: *Who cares! Let's run away from here and leave Albert all alone.*

Hayley: *Yes, yes, you are much nicer. She said my mum reminded her of a vampire. I am not going to ever forgive her.*

Laura: *If we go now she will stay hiding behind the couch forever until Val vacuums her up like a disgusting ball of dust. Shit and other swears. I am a bad girl.*

Hayley: *Let's go and be bad together.*

Fin.

I felt a light tap on my shoulder.

'Hey, oi!'

I sat up.

'Um, so Hayley is still outside. Sorry. He was all serious and said he needed to talk to you and that it was important.'

'No,' I managed to whisper before bursting into tears. I wanted to be alone but I was also taken aback by Laura's kindness. I expected her to push me out the door as soon as Hayley knocked. It wasn't as if she was ever cruel. She behaved much like me when I'd had too much sugar at a party. After I got into so much trouble on Christmas Day, I never wanted to be so obnoxious ever again. I hated myself for acting like that, but I never hated Laura for it. How come I loathed certain qualities in myself, yet adored the same ones in Laura? She was so much like me, except she was seemingly fearless and so earnest it was often unsettling.

'Al…Al, what's the matter?'

'Shouldn't we figure out —'

' — he can wait. He needs to learn to wait. Daddy Jonathan is awful at it. He starts tapping the steering wheel the second he stops at a red light and goes "shit, shit, shit" and scratches his head really hard which is probably why he's starting to lose his hair. Hayley can *wait*.'

I sniffed and rubbed hard at my eyes. As much as Laura was trying to act nonchalant about the boy at the door, she wasn't entirely convincing. She was flapping her arms against her sides with a kind of frenzied delight. I grabbed her by the wrist and she let me pull her down onto the floor in front of me, as if she had been reminded that my distress should be her central concern. She knelt and looked at me with wide eyes, awaiting instruction.

'I don't know what to do,' I said, my hand still tight around her wrist. 'I'm scared – but I need to talk to him as well.'

'Well,' she thought for a moment, 'I can tell him we'll go over to his place later maybe? You know how to get there? I'll come with you.'

I nodded, wiping a stream of clear snot onto my forearm leaving a glistening trail. I didn't want to go at all, but I needed to make sure Hayley and everything surrounding him — his parents, the Montereys, were safe.

Laura put a thick strand of her hair into her mouth and sucked on it hard.

'You know how to get to his house? I mean can we walk?'

I nodded.

'Right. Wait here.'

I placed my fingers back in my ears.

She was back in seconds.

'I asked him if we could meet him at his place. I said we were in the middle of something important, by the way, not that you were sad. So yes, I told him we need to have morning tea and a Milo which is true because I always need Milo in the middle of the morning and that we would walk to his house after that and he said okay.'

Janus padded up to us and Laura dragged her onto her lap. The cat twisted and turned, letting out a deranged mew before leaping free and scampering away. Laura laughed and held out her forearm. There were three long raised scratches.

'Stupid cat.' She sighed and closed her eyes and began repeating a bizarre little mantra to herself: 'A lung is a heart is a heart is a lung is a brain. A brain is a heart is a lung is a brain.' Then: 'He said to meet him outside the Garage in an hour. If you need to talk about anything private, I'll just be you – put my fingers in my ears and go *lalala*.'

I exhaled loudly.

'Can we have Milo now?' I wasn't allowed Milo at home.

12 / VIDEO NASTY

Most people on our street liked to personalise their mailboxes. Ours was a giant wooden oblong slathered with a thick coat of the same dark green paint as the house with a messy white number eight slathered on the front just under the slot. It was prone to liberally handing out splinters if you were too careless in lifting the flap at the back. Mother Ann eventually sanded it down and painted it sky blue, and the rest of the house would eventually follow.

On our walk to Hayley's, Laura and I took note of the eclectic mailbox art on display: psychedelic daisies, a fleur de lys (French), a metal milk bottle turned on its side to make the body of a cow with wooden appendages glued to it in a careless fashion.

'That milk boddle they turned into a pig wad better,' said Laura, sucking hard on a raspberry ice block, her words coming out all sticky, and with such urgency she didn't once consider removing it, 'Ye know de one just ad you're leaving town? De top of the boddle, de lid, ith de snout.'

I was too nervous to eat my ice block. I'd just had a glass full of six tablespoons of Milo so I was feeling a little queasy as it was. I didn't want to vomit in front of Hayley. After the watermelon incident I was terrified of vomiting in front of anyone again. I'd seen Hayley covered in dead horse and mud and snot but if I were to vomit — I just wasn't supposed to. Girls don't have fluids. Girls are filled with nothing but a temperate air. Melvin had told us he left a woman he was dating for throwing up in his bed. My icy pole was melting. Red syrup began running down my hand. I started to breathe heavily. Laura had finished her ice block and was now chewing the end of the stick. When she removed the end from her mouth it looked like the end of a tiny straw broom.

'It's fine just chuck it — you don't have to eat it.' She took the melting mound from my hand and tossed it into someone's front yard as we were passing, wiping the juice on the side of her mint green shorts, staining her flanks pink. She urged me to walk faster for a little while in case we were caught, reprimanded for such brash littering. When Laura deemed us safe, I stooped down to wipe my hands on the grass but it only attracted all the dirt and other detritus that dwelled in the undergrowth. 'Oh, Al, you stupid,' she laughed.

'You stupid' was the phrase Laura used when I failed to make a logical choice, when I acted out of panic rather than common sense. I was a joke.

'Never mind, Hayley's grotty, it's not like he'll get all snobby about it, we'll use his bathroom when we get there. Also – I've got blood on my pants,' she wiggled her hips from side to side showing off the stains on her shorts. The little butcher.

'But what if we're not allowed in?'

'You and Hayley and your weird families. We'll find a tap, he's got to have a tap in his house, right?'

I spent the rest of the walk picking grit off my hand, the juice drying like glue in the January heat. We arrived outside the Monterey's and Laura started laughing hysterically.

'Woah, ugly horse box!' The Monterey's had a smaller mailbox than most. It was one of a traditional style, with a metal stick attached to the side, but instead of the usual red flag on top there was a small, round two-dimensional horse.'Ha! look at Fatty,' Laura chuckled.

I shushed her. I was terrified that the Montereys would hear us and come out in a rage. I imagined a pair of fit, middle-aged riders in jodh-purs, brandishing whips. Maybe they had heard of our littering offence. Maybe the news had travelled via phone down the road as we walked and an angry mob was gathering to force us to clean up the entire street or else. Maybe we would stand accused of stealing the cross from the Monterey's gate.

I imagined all these furious, faceless people while Laura stood clasping both of her hands over her mouth trying to control her laughter, but still emitting frequent muffled, exaggerated snorts. The little, fat horse was rather amusing. It had an enormous round body and tiny limbs with white spots on its rump.

'What breed is it?' Laura sniggered through her fingers.

'Umm… Palomino Appaloosa Fat Face?' I let out a nervous giggle.

Laura started cackling again. I shushed her again. She closed her mouth and allowed a long, smug grin to spread across her face. She looked not unlike a cartoon frog. I wanted to tell her about the missing horseshoe cross, but then I would have to tell her about the dead horse and I had no idea how all these things were connected.

'Hey.'

We turned to see Hayley standing on the footpath across the street. It had been a while since I looked at him properly, up close. He was taller.

'Hallo!' shouted Laura, who immediately rushed over to greet him. Hayley shuffled his bare feet in the grass, impatient. Laura had launched into a rant about how amusing she found the Monterey's mailbox when Hayley interrupted.

'Um, you trust her?' he asked me. He looked terrified.

'Yeah, but she doesn't have to listen if you don't want her to.'

'No,' agreed Laura. 'I can block my ears and go *lalala*.'

'Mum's in hospital and I don't know why.'

Laura chewed on the corner of her thumbnail.

'Oh.'

'Is she okay? Is it the sleep sickness?' I had never had a loved one ill in hospital; I wasn't sure how to act.

He ignored the question.

'Dad's been away for days and I don't know when he's coming back.'

Laura looked down and began scuffing the ground with her sneakers. Like she was somehow unconsciously imitating Hayley. We heard muffled voices across the road. The Montereys were opening their garage. I could see that Mr Monterey had thin, silver hair and a large beer belly. Mrs Monterey looked severe. She had black hair with silver streaks pulled back in a tight bun. She wore large seventies-style eyeglasses on a chain and she lifted them to her face and glared at us as Mr Monterey started their four-wheel drive and she opened their front gate slowly, suspicious. Hayley rushed us around to the back door of his house.

The living room was still a mess. The couch where Helen usually lay was covered in towels and the coloured embroidery thread she used to make friendship bracelets was strewn across the armrests. Laura asked if we could use the toilet and Hayley told us he would be in his bedroom. He motioned towards a room just off the living area.

I followed Laura down the hall. The Durston's bathroom was cramped. Small mosaic tiles in various shades of brown covered the floor, and some were missing, especially around the toilet. Laura slammed the door shut and rushed to the toilet while I used the small vanity next to it to wash my hands. While I tried to lather up a dry cracked sliver of yellow soap, Laura sighed, shivering slightly.

'I needed to wee so badly.' She lifted her legs, her feet almost touched the shower cubicle opposite her, her shorts dangling from her ankles. 'I don't even care that this bathroom stinks of boys.'

She was right. As I moved my hands under the running tap I saw a surplus of hairs, long and short, stuck to the side of the sink and hoped Hayley wasn't thinking about our piss and our shit.

Hayley's room was a converted sunroom with orange textured glass windows running the length of it. The 'room' itself was only about a metre and a half wide. A single bed was wedged into one end, covered with a faded green chenille bedspread. On the wall above the bed was a poster that said: 'Texas State Animals', featuring illustrations of the official animals of Texas including the American Quarter Horse, the Guadalupe Bass and the Lightning Whelk.

'My uncle in Texas sent me that in the mail a few years ago.' Hayley's Uncle Jim, Helen's brother, owned a printing press in Austin, specialising in educational and government posters. Hayley was always talking about how one day he was going to live with Uncle Jimbo in Austin. Though he had never met the man, he had an unshakable idea that America was a better place to live.

Laura motioned towards another poster that read: 'Who will survive and what will be left of them? *The Texas Chainsaw Massacre*.' She demanded to know where he got it.

'Barry at the video shop gave it to me for free,' said Hayley. 'He was cleaning up the back room and I helped.'

'Have you seen it?' I asked.

Laura's eyes went wide.

'Oh, oh can we watch it? Can we?'

'I don't have it. Never even seen it. I've got some other movies hanging around, taped off of TV. I'll see what's in the TV cabinet, but don't show your parents. I don't want your mums getting up my mum or anything.'

'I haven't got a mum; my dad is always out and doesn't talk much, it's fine.' Laura sat on the floor and hugged her knees to her chest like she was ready to tell him her life story.

'Yeah. Well, Albert, I needed to talk to you because, um, you know the Montereys? Well, they had a cross, made from horseshoes, on their gate.'

'Hey, should I go outside for a bit?' Laura asked.

'No you shouldn't. Dad might come back. Maybe. Look, I don't know, nobody has told me what's going on.'

'I know you don't know me…' Laura began.

'You can trust her,' I said, a little too sombre, sitting on the floor beside Laura, who nodded in agreement.

Hayley sat in front of us as though he was about to perform in front of the world's smallest crowd. He turned first to Laura.

'A while back, we were in the paddock out the back and we found a dead horse.'

Seeing Laura unfazed, I continued the story in an urgent, subdued tone:

'It was awful and no one had come to bury it or anything. It had been dead for ages but Hayley doesn't know which one it was, I mean, what its name was, but it was one of the Monterey's horses, right? On their land? So, they aren't looking after their horses, they're really terrible people and you saw their mailbox and their front yard they're just weird.' I realised what I was doing and stopped. 'Sorry,' I told Hayley, 'you say it.' I told myself to keep my dumb mouth shut.

Hayley was just staring at the floor and there was a silence that felt like it was going on forever so I continued:

'Hayley, the horseshoe cross was gone after that, is that what you

were going to say? That's what I wanted to tell you, I saw it too. I'm
sorry I didn't tell you straight away but I thought that maybe it wasn't
such a big deal but it felt like a big deal but I didn't think...I mean,
Laura can still go it's fine.'

Hayley picked at his toenails. 'It's okay, she can stay.'

'Al and me are best friends,' said Laura, with pride.

I nodded.

'You should see inside her house.'

'Has she shown you her split thing?' Hayley asked Laura.

'Split uvula,' I corrected him.

Laura grimaced.

'That sounds gross and rude.'

'It's the dangling thing at the back of your throat. She's got two.
Show her.' Hayley insisted.

I opened my mouth wide and Laura peered inside.

'I can't see two it just looks all… swollen.'

I closed my mouth and coughed.

'They get stuck together sometimes' I said, feeling perplexed by the
intimate attention being paid to the inside of my body. I opened my
mouth again. 'Ya seet?' I asked, my jaw aching. Laura stared for ages,
making a series of sounds that were halfway between awe and repul-
sion. When I was finally able to close my mouth, she was still staring,
her stained lips parted slightly. I could see Hayley over her shoulder,
leaning his head back against the side of his bed with a grin on his face
that made him suddenly look like an adult. His cheeks were flushed.
They both looked beautiful. I know this memory is entirely selfish. I
think I found them so beautiful at that moment because they were both
in awe of me for the first time and it was at something so intrinsically
ugly, something I thought made me monstrous, that was actually a
source of fascination for them. I want that all the time.

'Al, that is amazing,' said Laura. 'That must make you special.
What does it mean?'

'It doesn't mean anything.' I would get annoyed with Laura
when she would suggest that every event, every new thing she experienced, anything slightly unusual, must be somehow otherworldly
or significant. But that sounds like hypocrisy, especially when we
were in the middle of a serious meeting about some vulgar

ephemera disappearing from the front gate of virtual strangers. 'It's bad Laura, I almost had a hare lip, which is when the whole top of your mouth splits and you end up with a kind of line like a rabbit does, under your nose. I was almost deformed. It's not a special thing.'

'Weird.' Hayley grinned.

'No, no, no. It's a sign,' Laura stared intently at the floor, thinking.

'Of what?' Hayley asked.

'I'm not sure yet.'

'I told you it means I was almost deformed. It's not a special thing, Laura.' I needed to change the subject. 'Do you know where the cross went?'

Hayley sighed. 'The cross is under our couch. It's been there for like, a year.'

'You're pretty bad at keeping secrets,' said Laura.

'Yeah, well I think Mum stole it. When I came home from finding the horse, Mum saw me, she was up, she was in the kitchen and she saw the mess.'

'There was blood?' Laura started sucking on her hair again.

'No, there was no blood left, I just had some mud on me. And some hair.'

Laura flicked her hair out of her mouth.

'I — I was trying to find out how long it had been dead for,' Hayley stammered, attempting to explain his behaviour. 'Mum made me have a shower and then I went to my room and she was sitting on my bed and she said: "They're killing the horses". She was so out of it she just kept on saying: "I'll fix it, I'll fix it." She said that about four times before she left. "I'll fix it."'

'Fix it how?' I asked.

'I don't know, I don't know anything but it's under the couch and now Mum's sick like she got caught and now they've made her sicker.'

Laura stood up.

'That witch and her dumb husband across the road? Well, if they're killing their horses, your mum must have taken the cross to warn them, to say "I know what you're up to you murderers" and they found out and made her sickness worse so she had to go to hospital.'

Hayley stood up too and started fussing with a pile of old toys next to his bed. Laura stood over me and put her hand lightly on my head. After a while, his back still to us, Hayley said:

'She threw up everywhere. It was the middle of the night. I was asleep and when I woke up the ambulance was taking her away and they wouldn't let me near her. When everyone had gone I had to clean the sick off the couch because it smelled and I lifted up the cushions and I could see through the springs —the cross was there, under the couch.' He turned, rubbing his eye with the back of his hand. 'Anyway, youse should go now.'

'What about my videos?' Laura whined.

Hayley led us back out to the living room. It smelled musty, like vinegar and mould. He lifted one of the cushions on the couch. Laura and I peered down through a veneer of dust and silverfish, through rusty springs. There was the Monterey's horseshoe cross.

'Bloody Jesus,' said Laura. I'm not sure if she was shocked at the fact that Hayley was telling the truth or merely expressing a general astonishment at the amount of garbage that had accumulated under the Durston's couch. Empty pill bottles, blister packs with old drugs crumbling out of the torn foil, tangles of coloured thread, wool, dried flowers, some broken incense sticks, a small pine cone, a green army figure crouched, shooting a gun, some AAA batteries, a rubber lizard, an empty packet of Samboy Atomic Tomato chips, a gumnut, a ball point pen, a business card for 'Holistic Massage by Tracey'. A familiar magazine: *Chop off my legs*. It seemed like a nest that had been deliberately prepared amongst chaos, a tangled nest in which to hide a rare, mythical creature.

'Are you just going to leave it there?' I asked.

He shrugged. 'I thought I should. No one will find it under here. The couch is Mum's spot, my spot too I guess. It's safe here. Dad never cleans so he won't see it.'

'Unless he's looking for some gross, old Panadol,' Laura said.

'Don't think that's Panadol,' Hayley said.

I thought again about the angry mob, ready to make a citizen's arrest, to lock us all away.

'But what if someone comes asking? Knocking on doors and stuff?' What about the litter police and Mrs Monterey with her angry face?

'Psht, they'll only do that if they saw something. I haven't lived here very long but I don't think people take much notice of stuff. They probably leave their doors unlocked.' Laura scoffed.

'Yeah we do, so?' Hayley began rifling through the cabinet under the television. 'Mum always says even though she's sick, she's strong. Here.' He handed Laura a video cassette with a blank label. 'Dunno what's on it but you can give it a go.'

Then, the following things happened and not necessarily in that order: we heard a key in the lock. Hayley led us in a panic out through the back door and told us to crawl under the barbed wire fence and keep running until we got home. Laura clutched the video to her chest and sprinted ahead of me.

Once we had turned out of Solstice Lane I turned back briefly and saw a man – standing very still – outside the entrance to the Garage. He had no distinguishable features, the setting sun shining behind him made it difficult to see anything but negative space where a man should be. I felt like he wanted to hurt us. In a panic, I screamed out to Laura who turned and screamed even louder.

We ran until we reached the door of Laura's house. Her t-shirt was torn from the barbed wire fence, and she was panting heavily, dirt on her face. We collapsed on the front lawn; sat silent for a while. I knew we needed to get inside before the toads came out, but we also needed to make ourselves look presentable for Valerie, so she would not suspect that we had been up to anything, that we were upset. Still, when we entered the house, pale and subdued and late. Valerie took my chin in her hand and gazed at my face intently as though she was trying to find Laura. Then, as though disappointed, she dropped her hand limply to her side and told us to clean ourselves up and serves us right for making ourselves sick on too much chocolatey drink. She led us up the stairs to the bathroom and ran us a hot bath even though we were sweating and it was the middle of summer.

'Hot water makes it all better.' Valerie was stern in her reassurance, swishing the water around with her hand as Laura made a brief escape to her bedroom to hide the video. She returned to the bathroom as Valerie was exiting, her hand shielding the side of her face. Laura quickly shed her clothes, her stained shorts, her torn shirt and joined me in the enormous claw-footed bathtub. I remembered the scratch Janus had left on her forearm that morning.

'Show me your scratch.'

Laura held her arm out. The wound was still red and raised. It was covered in dirt.

'Do I have some on my back too?' She turned around. There was a shallow cut about two-inches long near her right shoulder.

I touched the wound lightly. 'Yeah. You don't feel that? It's bleeding a bit.'

'Nope.'

I pressed down hard. 'You feel it now?'

She shook her head. She turned back around to face me. Pieces of dirt began to float around us amid a cloud of suds. The heat and lingering nausea were making me dizzy.

Laura nudged me.

'So who do you think that was?'

'I'm sorry,' I said. 'I made you look at him.'

'No...' Laura's words evaporated into the steam.

'No?'

'No...it's...we have to talk about this I know, I know. I just haven't told you.' Laura slid down so her head was the only part of her body not submerged. 'I've seen that — him, before.'

'What? When?'

'The day we moved in. Daddy Jonathan and I got here before those removal men. We had the keys so we went inside to wait for them and you know the window by the kitchen sink that looks out onto the back yard? '

I nodded. I sank further under the water too. As though it would protect me from what she was about to say. I couldn't bear the tension so I said it first:

'He was out there.'

'Yeah. And I was too scared to do anything. He just stood there for a while — well the shadow did, he was like a black shadow — and then he just disappeared. I didn't see which way he went. It was...I feel dizzy.'

'It's the water. Valerie made this too hot. We should get out.'

'Soon,' said Laura. 'It feels safe.'

'But I need to do something to stop thinking about this,' I pleaded.

'When I think too much about things they scare me even more because my brain makes them worse —'

'— but you've seen him too?'

I nodded. 'Yes. I mean probably. Yes. I had a dream about him. I think his name is Mister San Hosantio.'

Laura breathed in hard before disappearing under the water. I could feel the side of her body slide up against mine, like a slippery fish, her foot stopping close to my hip as she lay deathly still on the bottom of the tub. I did the same, being careful not to hit my head on the gold tap behind my head. I tried to lie as close to the bottom of the tub as Laura but the top of the bath plug and the chain attached ruined the sensation. Laura was still underwater when I resurfaced. I nudged her gently with my foot and she emerged, dark circles around her eyes, thick strands of wet hair covering her face.

'What?' she asked as though I had disturbed her slumber.

'There's nowhere to put my head. I don't know where to put my head.'

Valerie made us dinner, but we had little appetite between us.

'Bloody chocolatey drink. Bugger it,' she muttered as I stabbed listlessly at some peas with my fork and blew bubbles in my glass of water while Laura sat slumped in her chair, mumbling a monotonous unidentifiable dirge to herself.

'What's she doing?' asked Valerie, pointing in Laura's direction but staring directly at me.

'I'm singing, Val.'

'Don't be insolent,' Valerie snapped. At me.

Laura stood up and walked behind her. 'Hey, hey Val,' she whispered in her ear. 'Turn around.'

'I will not, I shall not, you shall be punished tonight, early bedtime, go on, teeth, now, bugger it.' I had never heard anyone in real-life use the word 'shall', let alone twice in the same sentence.

Laura hissed like a cat, spraying the side of Valerie's face with spittle.

Valerie's flat was attached to the ground floor of the house so when we were sure she had retired for the evening we snuck upstairs into Daddy Jonathan's bedroom. He had a small television at the foot of his bed with a VCR attached.

'We used to watch videos all the time,' said Laura, 'I mean, we still do sometimes, when Daddy Jonathan has time off. But we don't do it as much as we used to.' She fiddled with the remote control as I made myself comfortable on the bed. The bamboo-print bedspread smelled like a sweeter version of the Durston's bathroom. Of aftershave, minimalism. If minimalism had a smell. I imagine it is the opposite of the smell of old books. No man I have ever known has valued possessions. I thought Hayley cared about his Texas State Animals poster but I heard he tore that up after a while, so he probably never cared about anything either.

Laura was still reminiscing.

'Where we used to live, every Saturday morning we would go to the video shop and I could pick two videos then we'd go next door to Big Rooster and get a big box of chips —one each — and then we'd come home and watch the videos in bed and I would use the video case as a little table to sit my chips on and when I'd finished eating the video case smelled like it was alive, like sweaty skin and chicken salt. Movies smell like that, to me.' She sighed and pushed Hayley's video into the VCR, then reached under the bed to retrieve a large stick. 'Hey, see this?' She joined me on the bed. She lay the stick alongside one of the bamboo fronds printed on the bedspread. 'Daddy Jonathan is really into bamboo.'

'Why does he keep it under the bed?'

'Burglars. He really, really wants to hit a burglar. So, if this stick can hurt a burglar, it can keep us safe — if there are any scary things on this video.'

We slid under the covers. Jonathan's sheets felt starched and new. Unweathered, unsentimental. Laura pressed 'play' on the remote with one hand and placed the stick of bamboo between us on the bed with the other.

'In case we need it,' she said in a tone that was far too solemn for my liking.

We sat through almost a minute of static before anything appeared on the screen. Then, a film began, abruptly – from somewhere in the middle it seemed. It looked like it was made in the seventies. I was enthralled by the vivid red of the blood that flowed under doorways, down bedheads and from the eyes of the heroine who had somehow been blinded. She had woken from a fevered sleep and become an oracle who sees and yet does not see. A demon with a dragon's tail crawled across the ceiling. The woman's translucent nightgown, torn on one side, an exposed breast. A man with a white face leered at her through the window.

Laura lay her hand on top of the bamboo stick. I placed my own hand on top of hers and clutched it hard as our oracle heroine, having a disturbing precognition of the presence at her window, stared him down with her white pupils framed by perfectly exaggerated cat eye makeup, complete with powder blue eyeshadow. Blood flowed from her eyes faster and heavier and the music swelled as she thrust her arm through the window. From the outside of the house the camera zoomed in on her bloodied arm reaching out, frantically trying to grasp at something that wasn't there.

'I think she killed him,' said Laura. The ghost, I mean, or whatever he was.'

'She was pretty,' I said.

We sat in silence watching the commercials that followed. Then, a televangelist. I often wondered who, when I scanned the TV guide, were 'Kenneth Copeland' and 'Creflo Dollar Jnr.' and why they always held the 2am to 6am time slot every morning on commercial television. A woman with a large perm was espousing how the devil can trick you. That he wears many masks.

'I think Val watches this,' said Laura, yawning.

'Is she religious?' I asked.

'Nah. I mean she never talks about god and stuff. She just says a lot of weird things, about turning your back to the devil. She's sad.'

The blind oracle was a surprising comfort to Laura and me. We would go on to see many films like it, but that hour of theatrical techni-colour gore made us feel like we had control. To gain that control though, I had to sacrifice a little to Laura. We stayed awake that night, whispering together under the covers of Daddy Jonathan's bed, talking about how we would fight back against the figure that was haunting us. Laura was convinced that we had to go back to Hayley's and confront Mister San Hosantio. She suggested we blindfold ourselves and stand in the place where we last saw him. On the footpath outside the Garage and count to nine.

'Why nine?' I asked.

'It's lucky,' Laura whispered.

I must have fallen asleep then. Early in the morning I woke up to find Laura curled up at the foot of the bed clutching the stick of bamboo like a stuffed animal. She had taken all the covers off the bed and draped them over the television. I didn't want to wake her. I had a sudden, painful urge to be alone.

13 / SAMSON AND THE MILLSTONE

Laura told me she didn't put the bedclothes over the television and it wasn't at all funny to say she did.

We were sitting in class, cutting pictures out of a pile of old travel brochures. We were to research a capital city and make a presentation on it the following week. I was writing 'Tokyo' in bubble letters on top of a large piece of pink cardboard. Laura had smothered her hands in PVA glue and was waving them about so the glue would dry and she could peel it off. Her piece of cardboard was still blank aside from a small, crude pencil drawing of the Eiffel Tower in the top right-hand corner.

'Well, it wasn't me,' I said, a little too loud.

Our teacher called to us from the other side of the classroom to 'control our noise level.'

'I didn't,' hissed Laura, 'but I know you're not lying either.' She tried to peel some of the glue off her hand and made a face when it didn't come off in the long, satisfying strips she expected. 'So, we know who did it, then, don't we?'

I thought for a moment.

'Why would Val do that?'

Laura groaned. 'It wasn't bloody Val. Mister San Hosantio. Remember the last thing we were talking about before you fell asleep?'

'The thing. To keep him away. The blindfold thing.'

'And then what?'

'I don't remember.'

'You don't remember me saying we were going to go back there on Saturday?'

'No, I must have fallen asleep by then.'

'You said okay, you went, *yup*.'

'But I don't want to go back,' I said. 'Hayley probably doesn't want us to.'

'He doesn't need to know. We just have to go to the last place we saw Mister San Hosantio, okay? He was outside the Garage, on the footpath. You put a blindfold on me, you light the sage stick with a match, you put your blindfold on and I'll clean the area and then when…I don't know, I guess when we feel like the place is clean, we can leave.'

I told her fine, but it all sounded pointless. She responded with a long diatribe about how stupid the name Mister San Hosantio was and was I sure I didn't hear the name wrong? It was a dream after all, and it's easy to forget the details of dreams. I said I was sure, even though I wasn't. The pressure to commit to this ritual was far too high.

Daddy Jonathan was sitting on a bench in his back garden, reading an intimidating-looking novel.

'Daddy, we need to borrow your ties,' Laura announced. 'Two of them. They don't have to be new ones.'

'I don't own any,' he said, fishing about in the pocket of his bathrobe for his cigarettes.

'But we need them for a school play. In the play, we have to wear blindfolds.'

He squinted at us through a thick veil of smoke. 'Valerie,' he mumbled before returning to his book.

We made our way to Durston's Garage. Laura was wearing a backpack containing two of Valerie's cheap imitation silk scarves and some sage she had picked from the garden, rolled up in some newspaper and tied together like a fat cigar with some jute twine.

'Do you think that was Hayley's dad at the door? Do you think he came back?' I asked as we walked.

'Well who leaves their kid at home on their own after something so awful has happened? I mean Daddy Jonathan is the worst bastard but I don't think he'd do that to me.'

When we arrived at the spot we believed Mister San Hosantio had appeared, Laura opened her backpack and handed me a scarf.

'What if the Montereys see?'

Laura shushed me and clasped the sage in her hand.

'We've got to be quick, so hurry up and blindfold me.'

I did as I was told. Laura insisted on me tying the scarf as tight as possible. Then I took the matches and lit the end of the sage stick. The entire thing immolated in a number of seconds and Laura was left sucking her thumb. With her free hand she pulled her blindfold off and started screaming as the grass in front of us started to burn. We both tried swatting at it with the scarves but they caught light as well.

'I'm going to get Hayley,' said Laura, and ran off before I could protest. Who knew what would happen to her when she knocked on the Durston's door? What if no one was home and the blaze spread to the petrol bowsers? What if what if what if. What if I had just condemned a whole town to their deaths? I heard a chain rattle as the gates to the Garage opened. A surly, bearded man – who I could only assume was Bill Durston – marched out with a bucket of water, put the fire out, and left without saying a word. Laura ran to me, followed by Hayley, who locked the gate behind her.

'We're going to pick up Mum this afternoon,' he told us, through the wire.

'I don't understand what we did wrong,' said Laura, under her breath.

Valerie found out what we had done after Laura failed to return her scarves. She told Mother Ann, who forbade me from going to Laura's house for a month. When we saw each other at school, we poured through the reference section of the library trying to find out where we went wrong with the sage ritual. We couldn't seem to find any information about it.

'Where did you find out about this anyway?' I asked Laura.

'I don't remember, Unsolved Mysteries? It wasn't even sage, we didn't have any. I used parsley.'

When the month-long Laura ban was up, she phoned immediately and told me to come over.

'I phoned Hayley too,' she said as she opened the door, 'and his mum answered and she sounded really happy — like, completely cured and she put Hayley on and he didn't have much to say to me but his mum kept chatting really loud in the background, saying he should invite me over. She said it was a good time, she kept saying it until Hayley just went "fine come over today whenever" and hung up.'

I asked if I was invited too. Laura said of course, that because she and Helen had never met, it was likely Helen thought Laura was me. I said I wouldn't go. I didn't understand why Laura was so desperate to go back there.

'The first time we saw a ghost and then we nearly caused a petrol explosion.'

'If it's Bill you're worried about, I really don't think he's that bad. He could be mute. I didn't hear him say anything when the fire happened but at least he didn't do any yelling,' Laura reasoned, as though silence indicated placidity.

Daddy Jonathan also said very little, and he gave me a constant sense of unease. Father Robert was not much better. But at least he wasn't some monosyllabic chain-smoking intellectual. At least Father Robert sounded clever when he spoke and didn't stink of tobacco.

Laura continued.

'You know, Hayley's mum sounded like she really needed some girls to talk to. Could you imagine not living with any other girls and then going to hospital and coming back and no one has cleaned and your house smells of puke?'

Hayley led us into the living room with a reluctant yet somehow unspoken duty. Helen welcomed us through bleary eyes. She seemed heavily sedated, and quickly reconciled with the fact that there were in fact, two Albertas and one was named Laura. She offered to brush Laura's hair. I had heard from some other girls at school that everyone thought I did whatever Laura told me. I couldn't tell them I dreamed Mister San Hosantio first, that our hair was naturally the same, that we were both odd looking in our own way — so one day I tied by hair into a messy ponytail and cut it off just below the elastic with a pair of blunt kitchen scissors. What resulted was an asymmetrical mess that Mother Ann begrudgingly 'fixed' using scissors that were actually made for hair. I ended up with a frizzy pageboy that I would constantly wet to keep flat. I felt ugly and invisible at Helen's makeshift salon.

Helen was going at Laura's tangles with a comb, starting from the ends, telling her affectionately that even Hayley seemed to do a better job at keeping his hair neat.

'But I like to play with hair,' she added, 'It calms me. I even quite enjoyed it when Hayley used to come back from school with head lice. I like the process of it all. He, on the other hand, never understood why I didn't just shave it all off. But for some reason, Miss Laura, this is the knottiest hair I've ever tackled.'

'I tried doing that thing where you brush a hundred times before bed but it was so boring and it hurt my arm,' said Laura, wincing every time Helen dragged the comb through a knot. I don't know how she could stand it. I hate having my hair fussed with and pulled at. On the rare occasions I visit a hairdresser, I feel every follicle sting for hours afterward.

'You don't need to be that extreme,' Helen told Laura. I wanted to tell her that actually, yes, Laura did need to be that extreme.

'Dad's been talking about cutting my hair off,' said Hayley.

'When did he say that?'

'He's always saying it, Mum.'

'Can Mr Durston talk?' Laura asked.

I shot her a look that said: Stop it. Please stop. Stop now.

Helen didn't seem offended.

'He can, but he doesn't do it a lot. Only when he thinks it's important, but it's usually something we don't want to hear, isn't that right, Hayley Dean?'

I remembered seeing a film about a teenage boy with long hair whose father, a gruff soldier type, shaved it all off with a gold safety razor, the old-fashioned kind. I wouldn't put that past my image of Bill

Durston. He was clearly one of those military dads, who called his son a sissy and a pansy.

'Maybe it's a good idea,' Hayley said, 'but I'm not doing what he tells me.'

'How do you brush horse hair?' Laura asked.

'With a brush, dipshit.' Hayley lay on the floor, walking his dirty feet up the beige wall.

Helen chastised him. Laura looked hurt, as though she believed the rapport she was developing with Helen should have won Hayley's approval.

'I was just wondering because horses have really thick hair and maybe my hair wouldn't get knotty so easily if I used a horse brush.'

Hayley sat up and glared at me. As though I knew Laura's mind. As though I was suddenly needed to make the loud girl shut her face. *I don't know*, I mouthed at him. *Do something*, he mouthed back.

'Well, you could always go and ask the Montereys if they have a spare. They must have hundreds just lying around,' said Helen, suddenly fatigued, reclining back into the sofa.

'Mum!' Hayley stood up and glared at me again. I wanted to tell him to direct his anger at Laura, not me.

'She's not really going to ask them,' I said. I did wonder why, if it was true that Helen had it in for the Montereys, she was fine with Laura just knocking on their door.

Laura lay down by the couch and attempted to imperceptibly peer underneath. Hayley looked like he was about to reach down and drag her away when she suddenly pulled herself off the floor and announced:

'I'm going now.'

Helen was pinching the bridge of her nose as though she had a migraine on the way. Laura was about to stride out the front door when I grabbed her by the arm. She was laughing.

'Ha, like I would go out the front. We don't go out the front door here.'

Hayley looked terrified.

'Don't.'

'Let them be,' Helen sighed. Eyes closed. Then she mumbled something that I thought sounded like 'Won't go back ever again.'

. . .

Laura was determined to get herself a horse brush so as she entered the Monterey's front gate, I waited for her down the street, out of earshot, deliberating how I would, how I could act if she never came back. My mind alternated between scenarios of varying severity ranging from the Montereys laughing at her and shooing her off, to murdering her and leaving her dead body out in the paddocks to rot. I waited for what felt like half an hour before she came ambling towards me waving her hand that was strapped to a battered-looking equestrian grooming brush.

'Mr Monterey is really nice. He offered me some green cordial.' Then in a terrible British accent she added, 'I said, thank you, kind sir, but I must be on my way.'

I asked her if Mrs Monterey was there. Laura continued with the stupid voice:

'Mrs Monterey? Why, Mr Monterey said he's been a widower for twenty-five years, there is no Mrs Monterey, not here, not anymore.' She started to laugh. When she saw I wasn't, she reached over and tried to drag the dirty old brush through my hair.

I swatted her away.

'Was she there or not?'

'Not,' Laura replied, 'and I was glad. I don't trust her face.'

'But *he's* nice?'

'Nah I made that up too. I don't think they were home. I snuck around the back to the stables and grabbed this off the ground and ran.'

I wanted to shout at her. To tell her she was scaring me, that I couldn't keep following her into situations like this and she needed to stop making it worse by telling stupid jokes. But I couldn't because I didn't want to lose her. I believed that if I ever disagreed with her, if we ever genuinely fought, there would be no chance of reconciliation. I had so little experience with this kind of friendship that I thought if I tripped up once I'd be done. So I played the game.

'So, is the cross still under the couch?' I asked.

'Uh huh, there was a cockroach egg on it.'

14 / ALBATROSS

Rachael Gold was complaining that Justine Birch, the minister's daughter, had not replied to her letters for six months.

'I know she needs to make new friends at her new school but it's rude of her to just stop writing to me when she promised we could be pen pals and I used some of my best puffy stickers on that letter, too.'

'It doesn't matter because I'm your best friend now,' said Jessie Benson, a relatively new student who had immediately risen to dominance in grade five playground politics simply because she spoke her mind and demanded things and stood up for herself.

Jessie Benson did all the things we were told would serve us badly in adulthood —that being 'up yourself' was undesirable. If you merely said: 'I'm really happy I got that third-place ribbon at sports day' or 'I like my new shoes' or 'I'm quite happy with my face' it meant you were an egomaniac who needed a good dressing down. Jessie was an exception. We were all too frightened of her to suggest she jump back into the pit of insecurity with the rest of us. All she had to do was whisper into Rachael's ear and start giggling for Laura and I to stop questioning her actions.

The four of us were sitting in what was referred to as the 'scramble net'. It was basically an oversized hammock. Laura was staring into the distance at some of the boys in our grade playing hand-ball.

'Are you even listening to her?' Jessie prodded Laura in the arm with the toe of her sneaker.

'It doesn't matter,' said Rachael. 'It's not like I was talking about anything exciting.'

'It's still rude. Laura! Hey!' Jessie started clapping her hands in Laura's face. 'You're being rude. Stop perving.' Jessie narrowed her eyes and inspected the two boys. 'Do you like Michael Horner?'

I laughed.

'No, she definitely doesn't. He tucks his shirt into his shorts.'

'He pulls them up so high you can see what his balls look like,' said Rachael, who referred to any part of the male anatomy as 'balls'. Even an arse was balls to Rachael.

'Sam Walker's all right,' said Laura. She was somewhere else. It was like she'd become an answerphone playing a pre-recorded message, activated in the event the conversation turned to something dull.

Jessie started crawling out of the scramble net, making it rock from side to side.

'What is she —' Laura had switched back on.

'You said you liked Sam Walker,' said Rachael.

Laura looked incredulous.

'No, I didn't. I said he was all right, as in he's not a bad person.'

Jessie had marched up to Michael and Sam and started making exaggerated gestures and pointing in our direction. I told Laura she should probably try and stop whatever dreadful rumour Jessie was about to spread. Laura mumbled something like 'Jesus Christ' and flopped, unenthused, out of the net.

'I'm just going to sit here,' said Rachael.

'Me too,' I said.

'Like buggering hell you are,' said Laura, evoking Valerie for a moment, pulling at my arm. I rolled about in the net like a dying salmon.

'Laura, you're going to pull my arm off.'

She let go and ploughed on ahead. I limped after her as one of my legs had gone to sleep. We had been sitting in that stupid thing for at least half an hour.

'Woah,' said Michael Horner as we approached. 'Have fun getting bashed by girls, Sam.'

'Shut up, Michael.' Laura said.

Michael strolled off, making taunting cat sounds; hands in his pockets with the confidence of a middle-aged bank manager.

'Hey Sam,' Jessie was trying her best to look alluring in a pair of track pants with her sports skirt over the top. Around her neck she was wearing a velvet choker with a peace sign dangling from it.

Sam looked disoriented.

'We were playing a game,' he said.

'Yes, I know,' said Jessie, 'but I just wanted to ask if you would go out with Laura?'

Laura turned the kind of red that made me unsure whether she was angry or embarrassed.

'Actually, Sam, Jessie's just saying that because she's the one that wants to go out with you, but she doesn't know how to use words properly so I had to come over and do it for her. Sam, will you please let Jessie play with your—'

Jessie shoved Laura hard in the chest. Laura, in return, slapped her hard across the face and ran off towards the classrooms. Jessie watched Sam Walker creep away. Her mouth was agape as though she expected him to defend her. She turned to me, holding her stinging cheek with both hands like someone had taken a knife to her face and she was trying desperately to stop the bleeding.

'Are you going to hit me too? Or do you need her here to tell you what to do?'

She was half right. With Laura gone, I wasn't sure how to act. I wanted to stand up for us both, but she'd left me, and I was the one least capable of winning a fight. Laura ferried me about like a lame animal that would cower behind her at the first sign of danger. Rachael approached.

'We're not sitting with them anymore,' Jessie told her. 'So what are you going to do? Are you going to stick with me? Or the twinsies? The nutty town twinsies? Because if you're supposed to be my best friend and if you decide you like them better, I'll tell everyone what happened on sports day.'

Rachael, without any hesitation, swore her fealty to Jessie.

• • •

There was a niche under the stairs of one of the school buildings that Laura and I would squeeze into when we needed respite. It was our cold, concrete bunker. For security and the discussion of private matters. I found her there — more furious than sad, but it was the first time I had actually seen tears in her eyes. And over something that wouldn't usually bother her so much.

'Sorry,' I said.

'For what?' she asked, agitated.

'For letting that happen. I couldn't say anything. My mouth just felt all dry and gross.'

Laura lay down, using her backpack as a pillow; straightening the skirt of her uniform under her thighs to protect them from the rough concrete floor.

'It's okay, you didn't do anything wrong.'

I found myself increasingly in need of someone to tell me that.

'Rachael isn't going to sit with us anymore because Jessie said that if she didn't keep being her best friend she'd tell everyone about what happened on sports day.'

'What happened on sports day?'

'Only Jessie knows.'

Laura wiped her nose on the sleeve of her jumper.

'I don't know what the big deal was. I wasn't even looking at the boys, I was just staring into... nothing. I was thinking about stuff that had nothing to do with Jessie.'

'I know. Why can't you say a boy is a nice person without someone saying you want to be their girlfriend?'

'I don't even know if Sam is nice or not. I just said it for something to say. I wasn't really listening because I thought I saw something weird.'

'What did you see?' I felt obliged to ask the question.

'I dunno, there was just some weird kind of yellow light coming through the trees behind the handball court.'

'Sounds like the sun,' I said. Her superstitions were starting to bother me. I didn't want to talk about violent fables all the time. I didn't want to create any more of them, at least. But then, Laura sat up.

'You know, Rachael said before I moved here, there was a girl that died.'

I realised I hadn't even thought about Philomena Rankin's death since Laura showed up. It didn't feel like a memory I had merely put aside, it felt like one that had been erased and returned. I could hear Laura asking me what was wrong but she sounded far away, like the sound of waves in a seashell – you're not sure if it's actually there or not. Laura had to physically shake me to get me to respond.

'She did. She died.' I told her the whole thing. Even about the stupid rumours about the furnace and spontaneous human combustion.

Laura knelt down by the furnace and inspected the offerings to Philomena, all covered in a layer of dirt. No one had paid their respects in a while. Laura examined some of the objects — a marble, a trading card with Batman on it, a single sock.

'So she was your first friend? When you moved here?'

'No. She was mean. I didn't want her to die but... she wasn't my friend.'

'But what if she didn't die? What if she said sorry and you became friends? Maybe then, I wouldn't even be here.'

I asked her what made her think that.

'It's just one of those scratching feelings. I get them in my chest. When something doesn't feel right. Like when Janus scratches me, but it feels like it's coming from the inside. It doesn't really hurt, it's just a kind of sting.' Laura took a blue clip out of her hair and laid it at the foot of the furnace.

We both felt the pain of disenchantment. School had become dangerous, filled with ten-year-old girls learning about being a teenager, who were, for some misinformed reason, desperate to be sixteen like the thirty-year-old women that played them on television. Feeling like dating boys by sending them a note and asking them to tick a box and then never speaking to them for a day and then sending them another note to say they were 'dumped' was more important than anything else. There were a million complex forces coercing us into an early adolescence and I couldn't tell if it was impatience for sexual experience or a subconscious idea that our innocence would be destroyed sooner rather than later so we might as well throw ourselves into the mire — to begin experiencing pain and confusion as early as possible in order to soften the blow before the real burdens of adulthood rendered all these little awkward interactions inconsequential.

I could already tell that Laura and I were becoming less honest with each other. The stings just piled up on us. Stuck to our backs like arrows, each one randomly releasing a dull, persistent ache that we responded to in ways that I originally thought so dissimilar: she would talk, I would hide. That's how it worked. But when she needed to hide too, what then? I was convincing myself I needed help more than she did. I imagined that one day I might snap and start behaving exactly like Louis, tearing up books with my teeth and bashing my head against the wall. But I couldn't. There wasn't room in anyone's life for an Alberta like that.

15 / AFTER-SCHOOL SPECIAL

Mother Ann likes to tell me I can't take criticism. She told me recently that anyone can change their behaviour if they try, 'except maybe your father'.

'But I'm just like my father,' I said. 'I never leave the house, I can't do anything for myself and I want to die.'

She hates it when I say that. It's difficult when you so desperately need to tell someone how you feel, but you must not say precisely how you feel, because that wouldn't be very nice would it? Poor Mother Ann with the daughter who wants to die. It reminds me of a time not long ago when I was crying and screaming and hyperventilating and Mother Ann must have called Ma because she didn't know what else to do and I found myself, paralytic with distress, being lectured by my grandmother to 'smarten up' because I was 'upsetting my mother'.

I'm not saying Mother Ann should know what to do in these situations. But, frequently, in her desperation after one of my meltdowns she presents me with a list of things to do that might make me feel better in the future, such as going to bed at the same time at night, waking up at the same time every morning, taking more Vitamin B, taking my medications at the same time to make sure they work properly, walking Camille, doing some 'light yoga'. I try and explain to her that I have an innate inability to do these things and that it is not my fault.

I don't believe in constructive criticism when it comes to human behaviour. Criticising someone's ability to exist in a world that does nothing to accommodate them, that vilifies behaviours that are beyond their control, is never constructive.

'I'm attacking your illness not you' is often Mother Ann's response to this argument. I wonder, then, why she doesn't 'attack' Louis' symptoms? You can never convince him to do anything he doesn't want to do. Accommodations are made. I have to adapt. Just because I don't scream and moan and hit if you piss me off doesn't mean what I have isn't serious. My illness is not corporeal, it has no feelings and it won't go away if Mother Ann or Ma suggest I am not an active member of the household.

I can't even say half of these things to my mother. Even if I address them from what I believe is a very rational, logical position. Because when I cause a problem, that tips the scales. She can remain stoic when dealing with Louis but as soon as I become in any way confrontational, she starts to cry. I never once saw her cry when I was a child, but as soon as I became a difficult adult, she just couldn't hide it any more. I hate seeing my mother cry, but sometimes I can't comfort her either. Louis was the only one allowed a temper. Another tantrum from me was always just too much.

Whatever is happening with me, the thing, the diagnosis no two specialists seem to be able to agree on, needs to be controlled for the sake of everyone else. My sickness surfaced after Father Robert's 'phobias', after Louis' 'diagnosis'. I was supposed to be the normal one.

When I was eleven years old I accused Pa of being a sexual predator.

Laura and I had been discussing whether or not Hayley was being abused by his father.

'If Bill's doing anything to Hayley,' Laura said, 'he's hitting him, not molesting him.'

We had recently seen a movie about sexual abuse. I recall the crack of light shining through a door and a young girl's father — an imposing drunken silhouette — enters her bedroom. A bottle of beer placed on a pink shelf, next to ragdolls and teddy bears. Fat, hairy hands unbuckling a belt. Laura pointed out the father in the film did bear a resemblance to Bill Durston.

'Big, hairy, sweaty type. It's always truckers. Or plumbers.' Truckers punch their sons and shave their heads and rape their daughters. All of the bad men in Laura's head drove trucks.

Later in the film, the abused girl discovers her period is late.

'Shit, is it even possible for your own dad to get you pregnant?' Laura asked. 'Isn't there something your body can do to stop that happening? God, I'm getting cramps just thinking about it. You know they say childbirth is like period pain but like a million times worse? I mean I don't know what cramps feel like yet but you know what I mean.'

Laura couldn't stop talking about periods. When I started mine, she'd check obsessively for brown spots as I'd described them to her. I was secretly pleased I had beaten her to it but I was not enjoying the process. It started with a sharp pain in my nipples. I inspected them: it felt like a hard disc, like a checker piece, had lodged itself under each one. I could even move them around a little but it hurt. I told Mother Ann and she swiftly took me to get a training bra because our school uniform was far too see-through for her liking. I thought of Carly Simon and Linda Ronstadt and wondered how they could stand people seeing their nipples through their shirts. I thought of the blind oracle. She had small, fully developed breasts but her nipples were puffy like mine. All the women in the horror movies Laura and I watched had breasts that stood to attention, firm buttocks, excellent postures, everything was upright and looked great covered in blood.

I didn't like being looked at, I didn't like being under scrutiny. All I wanted was for people to listen to me and acknowledge that I was good, that I was present, that I was valid. Not that my body was changing. Especially when Ma and Pa came over to our house and as they were leaving Pa patted me on the arse and told me I was growing up fast. No one else seemed to notice this. Over the coming weeks, as I stewed and languished in the memory, I convinced myself he had done much worse in the past, that my memories had become repressed. I saw that on an episode of Oprah when I was home sick one day. That hallway light and the crackle of a beer can. These fears were soon confessed to Laura, after we saw Linda Blair in *Born Innocent*. Thrown in a female juvenile detention unit, some girls rape Linda with a broom handle. Another one of Hayley's late-night tapes.

'Tell your mum she needs to know how gross her dad is.'

'I can't. She won't handle it. Imagine if you found out your dad was a truck driver.'

'She can handle anything. She's the strongest lady I know.'

I agreed, but it was possible that one more family problem would break her. I tried to forget it, avoided kisses on the cheek from Pa and refused to talk to him until the situation became exceedingly tense one night when we were over at Ma and Pa's for dinner.

'Nearly finished grade six eh?' said Pa, a mouth full of spaghetti, his thin mouth stained with sauce.

'Why are you so excited about that?' I asked.

Mother Ann looked at me, ready to chastise me for being less than civil to my elders.

'Well, you know, not long before high school. Growin' up fast.'

The words came out of me as spontaneously as Laura's slap across Jessie's cheek: 'Some men like them young don't they Pa?'

He dropped his fork onto his plate in disbelief. It was almost the mirror image of Uncle Lyle after I said 'fuck' at Christmas, but this felt like another level of fury. His face seemed to bloat and expand. His jowls shook and he made indecipherable grumbling noises.

Ma and Mother Ann were making similar noises of confusion and disapproval in the background, but I was fixed on Pa's thin, grimy lips that he licked, probably from nerves, at the most inopportune time. I wanted to throw up; all those dirty jokes he told, all the times we just let him comment on the bodies of women on the television. The way he smelled of Tiger Balm and methylated spirits.

'You're an abuser!' I shouted, throwing a salt shaker against the wall.

Mother Ann dragged me outside and I started crying and screaming and she smacked me hard on the back of my thigh. 'What is wrong with you?' she asked, sniffling, dabbing at her eyes with a napkin she still had in her hand from the dinner table. Not quite crying, but close. I could hear Louis yelling inside and Ma saying, 'Now, don't you start.'

'Get in the car,' said Mother Ann, running back to her baby.

She didn't speak to me until the next afternoon. I could tell she had to take a lot of time to figure out what she was going to say to me. As if she knew I was, if not completely right in my accusations, justified in my protest. She said Pa was just being old fashioned, that men were like that 'back in his day'.

'And you just let them do what they wanted? Like broom handle stuff?'

'Broom handle stuff? I don't know exactly what you mean, but yeah, we just ignored it, mostly. At least the words. You can't stop the words. But he is not abusing you, kiddo. I know it makes you feel uncomfortable but there's nothing I can do about it.'

'Why?' I asked.

She said she just couldn't that was why. And did I know that Pa lent her all that money for an extension on the house just so I could have my own room? I wanted her to say she would protect me, that she would kill any man that tried to hurt me even if it was her own father. I wondered if Helen wanted to kill Bill for the bruises we would see on Hayley's arm. The occasional black eye, the busted lip he had when I first met him that he attributed to roughhousing with the dog. I thought hard about whether to ask Mother Ann if she knew anything about it.

'How do you know if someone is getting hit?'

She asked me why. Did I know someone this was happening to? Was it Laura? I said it wasn't. Then I had to tell her that we'd visited Hayley a few times and his dad seemed mean.

'Alberta,' Mother Ann started, slowly. 'What do you know about the Durstons?'

'Nothing besides what I just told you. But you can't tell anyone because it might not be true and Laura and I could get into heaps of trouble.'

Mother Ann nodded sagely and said Hayley might need to spend some time away from home.

I had been given the task of asking Hayley if he would like a job in Pa's new shop. I hated the idea and hated even more the fact that I had to arrange it. Sort of. Laura had to make the phone call. She spent a long time talking to Helen before she even brought it up. But apparently, when Helen called Hayley into the room to ask if he wanted to make some money, he said yes immediately. He wanted to start saving so by the time he finished school he could fly to Austin to live with Uncle Jimbo.

'At least Pa won't smack Hayley on the arse,' Laura said.

I told her not to be so sure.

Pa's shop sells fruit and vegetables and is called Byrne Family Grocers. 'Family Owned and Operated' the sign says. That isn't true. None of Pa's staff are family and I avoided going there as much as I could after the grand opening. Aunt Julia and Uncle Lyle came up especially for the event and Bethany locked me in the cold room for what seemed like an hour. I've never understood why country people feel the desire to emphasise the hereditary nature of their establishments. Are we supposed to assume that when we enter a family-run store the wares will somehow be superior? That we would receive the loving care and attention to customer service that was so lacking in those nasty city chains? You know, the ones where as soon as you enter you are set upon by a group of ruthless barbarians for daring to assume you could buy a crate of mangoes? Melvin Clemence's health food store was dreadful (it did indeed smell of carob and sprouts) but at least the name wasn't as misleading. It was called 'Organic Things'.

I knew it was a good opportunity for Hayley, but it also felt like in the aftermath of my accusations against Pa, I had been replaced by the grandson he never had. Louis didn't count because Pa had never once tried to engage him in conversation and if Pa was such a 'product of his time' as Mother Ann claimed, then it was likely he held the opinion that children like Louis should be sent away to an institution, shoved into a straightjacket and tied to the radiator.

Pa would ruffle Hayley's hair and call him 'son' and 'mate' and asked questions like 'Did you get that shiner at footy Hales?' Like he expected him to reply: 'Oh no! You have it all wrong! Dad got into a drunken rage and broke a bottle of Jack Daniels over my head!' Pa probably dreamed of exposing the parental neglect that the whole town had been whispering and tutting about. Pa would have loved nothing more than to gain custody of the poor little waif and finally give him the life he deserved.

Haley hated 'going to market'. He told me so, but he still went when Pa asked. 'Sure Mr Byrne!' he would chirp like a compliant scamp from a nineteen-fifties sitcom. 'Market' was, I gathered, where they got the fruit and vegetables from and going there meant getting up at some ungodly hour and driving there in Pa's ute. Most days, Pa would give Haley some fruit to take home and I imagined it sitting on the kitchen bench weeks later, still in the plastic bag, rotting.

16 / THE CRAWL

Hayley bought himself a new bike for his thirteenth birthday. He said his old BMX had been stolen. Thinking she would be amused, I suggested to Laura that maybe Helen had stolen his old bike and hidden it somewhere. I deemed it to be the kind of thing Laura herself would say. Instead, she admonished me.

'That's terrible. Don't you understand that Helen hasn't been sick since she stole that cross?'

I wouldn't say I had noticed a miraculous cure. To me, Helen seemed to always be either heavily sedated, drunk, or both. I did have to admit she hadn't been back to hospital since, but Laura didn't believe in mere coincidences.

'Sometimes you just have to remove one thing to make things better,' Laura said, like she was the presenter of the world's most vague self-help video.

Beyond the bushland that covered the Monterey land behind Hayley's house, there was a small creek. Hardly a rambling blue, cinematic river, it was a shallow, brown trench, full of sharp rocks and algae. We tried our best to swim in it, regardless. Each of us in our own way felt deficient, lacking in the wholesome vivacity of other children yet we did our best to emulate such an idyll, and tried to make the mundane seem alluring.

Laura was telling Hayley that even though his new bike seemed more 'mature' that didn't mean he couldn't decorate it the same way he did the last model. She said she liked to look at all the stickers, she said she would miss the ugly green skeleton with its tongue hanging out and the dog doing a poo and Jesus on a skateboard. '

Gonna get some Spokey Dokeys?' she asked.

Hayley said he didn't know what they were and Laura had to explain they were little coloured beads you put on your spokes that moved around and made a noise.

'So like a girl's bike? Piss off,' he said.

'Oh go on, they're so loud you can't sneak up on anybody and everyone would come out of their house to see you riding down the street and they would stare and stare and Al would hate it.'

I tried to ignore her, swirling my toes in the creek, imagining a life in sepia. Laura lay on her stomach next to Hayley's bike, stroking the metal frame with the backs of her fingers. At one point she leant over and let the tip of her tongue touch it and immediately screwed her face up at the metallic taste.

'Did you know that my grandmaman knew this artist…'

'Was this back in France in the Olden Days?' I asked.

'This was in America,' she answered, running her tongue over the roof of her mouth sitting up, cross-legged. She was wearing a green one-piece swimsuit with a small hole in the chest that could serve as an accurate target if anyone wanted to shoot her straight through the heart. 'US of the A.'

Haley was sitting on the opposite bank with his back to us, fumbling with twigs. 'Which state?'

Laura raised her voice significantly, craning her neck in his direction, like a little girl trying to impress her parents with amateur acrobatics. Look what I can do.

'Texas.'

Haley stood up and attempted to kick the twigs he was playing with away with his bare foot. Some of them rolled away, some toppled slightly into the creek and floated on the surface. Algae immediately began to attach itself to them, creating a green outline. He walked across the creek towards us. At its deepest, the water reached just below his knee. I tossed a towel at him when he reached us and he shook his head at me and let it fall to the ground as he went and sat beside Laura.

'Texas, yeah? How long did your grandma live there for?'

'Oh, she didn't! She was on holiday…it was summer, in Nineteen… Forty-Four.'

Haley grinned. 'Nice, World War Two.'

'That's not nice,' I frowned.

'Well it's interesting. We're learning about it in history, you know, in high school, where the mature kids with intellect go.' He was getting increasingly aware of his lack of general knowledge and would often call Laura and me smart arses when we corrected him on something. I was getting frustrated with his defensiveness.

'You used to ask me why, Hayley.'

'Why what?'

'Before, if I had said to you that World War Two was not nice, you would have been interested and asked me why.'

'Bullshit.'

'It isn't, you said I was smart.'

Laura didn't seem to care and carried on with a clearly fabricated tale about her grandmother escaping Hitler on a navy vessel and bribing sailors to do funny dances for her and when they arrived in America she got a lift into town on the back of a poultry truck and fell in love with a sculptor.

'Why was Hitler chasing her? Like actual Hitler — why would he decide to chase your grandmother all the way to America?'

Hayley rolled his eyes. 'She means the gestapo.'

Laura nodded vigorously. 'So they got married in Texas –'

' – where in Texas?' I interjected. 'Texas is a massive state. What city?'

'It was probably Austin, where Uncle Jimbo lives,' Hayley was still wide eyed and enthused, prepared to believe every stupid word that came out of her mouth.

'Yeah, yeah it was. And there was this cowboy —'

'— your grandmother never went to Texas.' I couldn't restrain my frustration any longer. 'You always tell the most stupid lies.'

Haley stared at me, then lowered his voice and said:

'Alberta you're not that smart. Just shut up.'

I felt a pain inside my chest, the scratching Laura had described. Then an ant bit me behind my knee and it set me off.

'It's true, she's always lying Hayley. And, what is that? *Alberta*? You never called me Alberta before Hayley *Dean*. Jesus.' I scratched savagely at the ant bite.

Then, a Laura Intervention:

'No blaspheming, Al.'

I would say that when you are on the edge of adolescence, the stinging sensation that fills your eyes when you're about to cry is the strongest it's going to get. That is, until you're close to death. I suspect when you're very old and alone it burns so much that it's what they've come to call dying of 'natural causes'. It's the sting that gets you in the end. I stood up to leave, smacking Haley across the face with my backpack as I passed him. I couldn't tell if it was an accident or deliberate.

'Watch where you're walking you annoying lump of shit,' he called after me. A wave of unfamiliar initiative came over me. I walked back to where he was sitting and smacked him in the face, with my hand this time, the same way Laura hit Jessie Benson. In return he punched me hard in the side of the nose and I fell backwards into the dirt and Laura screamed at me to piss off and fuck off and stay away forever.

I started crying in great heaving, choking bursts. I curled up on the ground, foetal. I heard Hayley say 'leave her' as though Laura was considering helping me but soon I knew she had left me too. It may have just been a small drop from my nose mixed with the tears but I felt like my mouth was full of blood, giallo blood, from an old Italian horror movie, the chocolate syrup Hitchcock used in Psycho, that covered our precious lady oracle, I felt it all overflow. I wanted my injuries to be severe. Ideally I could wear them forever, to show how I felt inside every single day. I wanted to be covered in blood, I needed everyone to see it. I would crawl my way back through the bushland bent and twisted and furious.

I told Mother Ann I had fallen and hit my nose on a log. I went to bed for a fortnight. I would lie there staring at the ceiling, my whole body becoming numb and transcending itself in my imagination to something small and insignificant. These kinds of thoughts sometimes give people comfort but it made me terrified. Who structured my existence? Was there someone else in the world, in the universe, called Alberta Howard who felt the exact same way at this moment? The thing I had feared most since Laura arrived had happened. They had deserted me and I could not fathom how I was ever going to recover.

Mother Ann took me to the doctor. Whenever an adolescent becomes sad and tired, they diagnose you with glandular fever. Glandular fever means you are run down. In America, they call it 'mono'. You wouldn't remember this, Jennifer, it was back last summer when you had mono. Your lymph nodes go all puffy and you get your homework sent home so you don't fall behind.

After a month of mono, Mother Ann walked me inside the school gate. I stuffed my hands into my sweatshirt and balled the cuffs up in my fists to stop my hands from shaking. Our year six teacher, Miss Miller, welcomed me back, as though I had been gone a whole year and part of me was comforted by her soft creamy face and round wire spectacles. I didn't look anyone in the eye. I sat down at my desk. I could feel Laura sit down next to me. I hugged my arms around my stomach.

'You got a stomach ache Alberta? Is that why you were away so long? Did you go to hospital?' asked a girl named Kirralee Jones who sometimes sat with us at lunchtime. She was one of those talkative girls that spoke to everyone, and treated them like a friend even though she never bonded with any one person.

I heard Laura sigh.

'Shut up, Kirralee.'

'I was being nice, Laura. Do you know what being nice means?'

I stayed curled in on myself for most of the morning. Then, Laura gently pushed a piece of foolscap paper across my desk. It was covered in the stickers she would get free with *Smash Hits* magazine and hide in the drawer under her desk and only use sparingly. Still, I could tell they were ones she didn't mind parting with. Neither of us were particularly fond of East 17 or Jeremy Jordan or Roxette. Underneath, in bright purple pen she had written:

• • •

Dear Al NOT ALBERTA I was at the supermarket with Val the other day and we saw Mother Ann and she told me how sick you were and was wondering if I knew anything about it and I said no and I don't think she believed me she looked like she was trying to be nice to me but underneath she was really really angry she said your nose was bleeding and you had a bruise on your head but I didn't see that Hayley was really mad and I thought he might hit me too or maybe get his gun out from the shed if I stayed with you so I went with him he hasn't talked to me since then he made me go home once we got back to his house and I wasn't allowed inside so I guessed his dad was there that it was a bad time like Helen says so I've been by myself for weeks Val has started learning to play the theremin which is like some kind of magic radio antenna that you wave your hands around and it is supposed to make music but it just sounds like screeching to me and it makes Janus so upset anyways I should be talking about you hey I asked Mother Ann if I could come over and see you and she said you wouldn't like that I hope one day you'll let me come to your house I don't mind about your brother or how much money your mum makes you've seen my stupid dad and psycho Val and Mel who is the grossest I don't think your brother could be that bad I know I make stuff up sometimes but not as much as you think sometimes when I'm lying I'm actually just making the truth more fun Uncle Mel says my stories are lively and cocettish I don't know how to spell that but I asked him what that meant and he said I am a natural performer so my stories they're not always lies they're not meant to make anyone feel bad there are things I believe that are true but sometimes I add some more interesting stuff so no one falls asleep I'm really bad at writing things down but if I was saying this to you in the way we usually talk then I could use my voice to show how sorry I am but you can't shout in a letter I was told by Mrs Curran last year that CAPITAL LETTERS ARE INCORRECT BECAUSE IT LOOKS AGRESSIVE BUT I DON'T CARE BECAUSE ONLY YOU ARE GOING TO SEE THIS BUT IT'S ACTUALLY HARDER TO WRITE IN CAPITAL LETTERS IT TAKES A LOT LONGER SO I'LL STOP thanks for not telling Mother Ann about what really happened anyway because I would have gotten into heaps of trouble I think Val sort of knows I did a bad thing but she wasn't even that mad she just said I should be grateful for you she says I should listen to you and she is right. I'm sorry. Can you still be my best friend even though I am an evil demon from hell please love Countess Laura the Third of Spain XXXXXXX

 ps it took me ages to write this it took like a week so I need to add this bit it

goes like this I was sitting in front of Hayley on the bus and told him how bad
I felt about everything and he is sorry too well he didn't actually say that he
was sorry he just kind of just nodded like he agreed with me he did say it is
good your nose was not broken and deformed for life he knows you aren't
supposed to hit girls he's a grotty turd but he needs us to be nice to him too.

17 / FAMILY TREE

Hayley stood in his doorway, scowling, as Laura began her peace negotiations. I noticed Helen had woven him a new bracelet. A belated birthday present, I assumed. He noticed me staring at his wrist and quickly put his arm behind his back like it was something to be ashamed of. Laura insisted that he apologise right that second.

I swallowed.

'No, it was all my fault anyway. I lost my temper. I've been feeling weird and I didn't mean to take it out on youse.' I thought if I subtly invoked his vernacular it would endear me to him again, but as soon as the word hit my lips I felt manipulative. I didn't like this new habit of imitation I had adopted. This whole ordeal started when I hit Hayley the same way Laura hit Jessie.

'Okay, well...' Hayley began as Helen emerged from the darkness of the living room and rested her long thin fingers on her son's shoulder. She waved at us with her other hand, smiling in a way I had never seen before. Hayley sighed and let us in. The smell of sandalwood incense filled my nostrils and made me want to sneeze but I pinched my nose until the feeling subsided.

Helen sat down on the couch and picked up a glass of red wine. She took a sip and smirked at us. 'Bill's off on a fishing trip with that arsehole Carl McKinnon.'

'Who is the arsehole Carl McKinnon?' Laura asked with immediate panic, as though she'd just been warned of another truck driver.

'You've probably never met him. He lives above the hardware store in town. He's older than Bill but they're such a bad influence on each other it makes me sick. But I shouldn't be complaining because my baby and I are cutting loose today, aren't we Hayley?'

'Yeah. We're cutting loose.' Hayley echoed in a caustic monotone. He sat beside her, arms crossed, staring at the floor.

'Oh, buck up sulky pants.' Helen nudged him in the ribs. This was the most animated Laura and I have ever seen her.

'You hate people telling you to buck up, mum, so why do you say it to me?' asked Hayley.

'Because you have the ability to do so. And I'm your mother and I can say what I like.' Helen was wearing a deep emerald green kimono robe, embroidered with red and yellow chrysanthemums.

Laura sat down, nervous but elated, next to her and gently fingered the corner of her sleeve.

'Was it expensive?' she asked, wide eyed.

'Cheap as chips. Used to sell them in my shop — when I had a shop. I still have a few in my wardrobe if you want to try them on?' She turned to Hayley. 'You too darling. Would you like to be a lady of leisure with us?'

He groaned and stormed out of the room.

Helen took another sip of wine and looked at me, like she knew I needed the attention. '

You wait for it...' she held her index finger up, her eyes glancing sideways out the living room window. Soon the yellowing lace curtains and the flimsy rail holding them up started to rattle and an intermittent thud sounded against the wall below. '...and there we go. Kicks his soccer ball against the wall, helps him relax. Never played a game in his life but I like to think he does it for more therapeutic reasons.' She thought for a moment. 'I suppose it would have done my husband some good to learn how to release his anger in a healthy manner when he was that age.'

Laura nodded, looking up at her in awe, not quite sure what exactly she was agreeing with.

'Did you know Bill when you were thirteen?'

'We were both in the same year at school, got married when I was eighteen, never knew anything else.' As though she didn't want to dwell any more on the subject, Helen went to her bedroom and returned with an old suitcase full of clothes.

Soon Laura and I were waving our arms about in the enormous sleeves of Helen's excess imported stock. The robes were far too big for us, of course, but we felt like shining, exotic birds. Laura in red with white cherry blossoms, me in blue with silver cranes. Helen poured us a small drop of red wine each in some plastic cups and put a finger to her lips.

'You're teenagers now right? A little of this won't hurt.'

'We're eleven,' I said.

'Almost twelve though, that's old enough,' Laura said, reaching for her cup.

Hayley's ball continued to thud against the wall. Helen leaned back into the couch with her new glass of wine and sighed.

'So what happened between you three? Hayley has been in the foulest mood the last few weeks. He's disturbing my... equilibrium. Is that what you call it? I've always liked that word anyway. Equilibrium.'

'Well...' I wasn't sure how to relay the events of that brief violent altercation by the creek without upsetting Laura again and criticising Hayley in front of his mother, 'He...we —'

'— did I mention I don't care what you say about my son? Did you think I missed the fact that he didn't actually tell you he was sorry?'

'Well he was sticking up for Laura really. I told her she sometimes makes stuff up and...' I turned to Laura. 'Sorry, it doesn't matter.'

Helen frowned. 'Do you lie often Laura?'

Laura looked pale. 'I...I don't mean to.'

'No, no, I know, you tell good stories. It doesn't matter.' I consoled her. I just didn't want to talk about it anymore. I had made it clear I had forgiven her, but at this point I desperately needed her to tell me something — just one thing — that was true.

'It does matter though,' Laura cried. She took a sip of wine, swallowed hard and made a sour face. 'I just want things to be interesting but then there are other times when I see things and people don't believe me.'

'What kind of things do you see?' Helen leaned forward. What was supposed to be my moment of redemption and reconciliation had become all about Laura.

'Shadows.' Laura sniffed.

'That's perfectly normal. I see them too.' said Helen.

'Are you going to tell them about Agnes?' Hayley appeared in the archway between the living room and the kitchen.

Helen swayed slightly and sighed.

'Yes honey but you aren't dressed for the occasion.'

'What? What happened to Agnes?' asked Laura, panicked.

'My grandma, not the dog.' Hayley said. Agnes the dog padded into the room (no doubt responding to the frequent use of her name), stuck her head between Hayley's calves and gave us a tongue-filled grin.

Despite his reluctance, Hayley must have taken his family lore seriously, because soon he was sitting on the floor in a green robe like his mother's while Laura and I sat on either side, braiding his hair. Agnes the dog lay on the couch with her head in Helen's lap, grunting with content.

Helen's family, the Kerrs, had been inhabitants of the area for four generations.

'Agnes Kerr, my mother, Hayley's grandmother, was born in this house. Her father was a dairy farmer, like most old families around here. Except Agnes had no brothers to carry on the family name and her younger sister, Vera, died of pneumonia when she was around the same age as you girls.' Helen drained her wine glass and poured herself another. 'So, when my grandfather could no longer run the farm, he sold all the cattle and started leasing the land out to horse owners in the area. That's why you see those old corrals, cattle enclosures around the place, all grown over and rusty. Agnes loved horses. But when Vera died, her mother wrapped her in cotton wool, told her a little girl who lived nearby — Ed Monterey's aunt, was kicked by a horse and became a vegetable so Agnes was never allowed near the things again.'

'Have the Monterey's lived here as long as your family?' I asked.

'Probably even longer. The old Monterey house where Ed grew up is still out there falling to bits behind their new place, the one he built when he got married.'

'Do you know the Montereys well?' Laura asked.

'Not anymore,' said Hayley.

Helen looked slightly taken aback.

'No, no not anymore. So Agnes stayed indoors all the time — it was rare for girls to go to school in those days — and she looked after her parents until they both passed. It was then once she was all alone, that Vera came back. Except she hadn't aged a day, she would sit in the corner of Agnes' room, with all the colour in her face as if she were still alive and told her that she wouldn't be alone much longer. Within weeks she was pregnant with me.'

We didn't get to hear the rest. Bill Durston rushed into the living room. He was wearing a white baseball cap that was covered in brown stains and faded text that read: 'The Pastime Club Truckee, California'. His face was swollen and flushed; his eyes small and porcine as he looked silently from Helen, to Laura, to me and to Hayley. His mouth twisted into a thin line of disgust. He grunted and stormed towards the kitchen where we could hear the clank of bottles and the slamming of cupboard doors. Helen sank back into the couch, closed her eyes and sighed. Like a machine that had been abruptly unplugged. Hayley pulled the braids out of his hair and ushered us out the door.

'It's fine.' He said, slamming it in our faces.

'What's fine?' shrieked Laura who began pounding on the door.

I heard a deep male voice roaring inside and I managed to pull Laura away as she asked many questions in rapid succession as we walked home. We were still wearing Helen's robes.

'Why did everything have to stop because big old Daddy was home? What did she mean her dead aunty made her mum pregnant? You know, Jesus, right? So Val — she isn't religious, but she likes to talk about the bible, or she likes to let people know she's read it. Anyway, Val said, when I asked her about baby making, that I wouldn't have to worry about that while she was looking after me because if I got pregnant it would have to be an immaculate conception. Like, Mary, she didn't do it with Joseph, it was just like, boom! Baby.'

'I think she was going to say Agnes met a man and he got her pregnant.' I said. 'That's how I saw it anyway. And I wouldn't ask. I don't think we'll ever be allowed back.'

Laura ignored that.

'Okay so, in that case, was Hayley's grandfather a Monterey? Agnes loved horses. Did you hear that part?'

I nodded. 'You're saying you think Ed Monterey is Helen's brother?'

Laura breathed out slowly as she processed this.

'Well — there was a Monterey girl that got kicked by the horse — but if she had a brother, then yeah…'

'But if no one knew who Helen's dad was, then it could have been anybody.'

'Yeah but they lived close together…now I'm getting confused,' said Laura.

'The Durstons and the Montereys weren't the only families living here back then. Plus in those days you could meet people that didn't, you know, live in your street.'

Laura went quiet. Our world was so mundane and insular that we couldn't perceive a world outside it. That there were people not in this town, not on this street. It was as though we had resigned ourselves to the fact we would never leave.

18 / MY BEST FIEND

In our final year of primary school, Laura insisted on wearing a full-length black leotard to school every day because she said it was what professional dancers do and she was going to be one. She said she couldn't breathe in the school uniform, that she liked the way the leotard completely covered her arms and legs. She said it made her look like a shadow. Maybe if she became Mister San Hosantio, maybe she could beat him.

One Friday, Melvin was supposed to pick us up as I would be staying at Laura's the night. Daddy Jonathan was away and Valerie was unavailable as, according to Laura, she had spent all night crying and puking at the same time and refused to let Laura help her.

While Mr MacIntosh —the teacher on pick-up duty that day — went to the office to call Melvin, Laura and I ran down to the playground. Laura hung by her knees from the monkey bars, humming to herself. I persistently asked her what the time was and shouldn't we be getting back and what if Melvin showed up and we weren't there and he went back home? We could be stranded. I couldn't find the strength in my arms to even swing from one rung of the monkey bars to the next.

'It's fine, it's fine,' Laura said, waggling her plastic digital watch at me as though the very act of wearing the thing put her in control of time itself.

Soon, Mr MacIntosh came blustering towards us, saying Melvin had forgotten all about collecting us and he was on his way and didn't we know that the playground was off limits after school hours and had we not observed the special stranger danger presentation Officer what's-his-face gave last week? He herded us back to the 'collection zone' — a fenced off area in front of the car park, covered in brown grass and pine needles. Laura peered through the fence with her matted eyelashes, wet from sticking her long hair under the drinking fountain to cool down. She would never admit how uncomfortable she felt in her leotard on hot days. When I suggested she at least roll the sleeves up, she shook her wet ponytail in my face, before sticking a wad of hair between her lips.

When Melvin arrived he immediately started chatting to Mr McIntosh like we weren't even there. Mr Macintosh was from Scotland. He was the music teacher and on Thursday afternoons every student from grades five to seven would shuffle into his room and sit shoulder-to-shoulder and sing (reluctantly) in unison to all the songs Laura and I hated and felt too old for as tetchy prepubescents, like 'Kookaburra Sits in the Old Gum Tree' and a horrible traditional Scottish song, about the banks of some loch and taking the high road and taking the low road. During these lessons, Laura and I would sit up the back with a wooden glockenspiel, carving star shapes into the wood with a compass point. Laura would do the engraving and I would fill in her indentations with felt pen.

Melvin and Mr McIntosh were talking about the local amateur theatre company. Melvin was the director. Mr McIntosh said he'd be interested in providing piano accompaniment for the next production.

'Look at his bug eyes.' Laura said of her uncle, crossing her arms. 'Big bug eyes. Do you think I have bug eyes? I had a dream the other night that I had these metal things holding my eyes in, to stop them falling out.'

'Sounds scary,' I said.

'No, I felt safe. They were like braces for your teeth except they were on my eyeballs, but I could see just fine.'

Laura had a fear of eyeballs and eyes falling out since she saw an experimental animation on television about a nuclear bomb exploding and a woman holding a baby got all burned up and her eyeballs fell out of their sockets. I think it was a British program, a product of the

Thatcherite era of cold war fear mongering around the impending nuclear holocaust. I told Laura her eyes were large but they didn't look like they were popping out of her face.

'They might when I'm old,' Laura frowned. 'Ugh, hurry up Mister Loch Ness!' Mockery, scorn, derision.

'Girls, sit back down in the collection area, thank you kindly,' he waved us away.

Laura stayed put, linking her arm in mine, twisting it awkwardly. She glared at Melvin.

'Going?' she asked, biting at her fingernails.

'Oral hygiene please, Miss Clemence.' Mr McIntosh sighed, motioning towards her mouth.

'Keep yer knickers on, love,' said Melvin. He turned back to Mr McIntosh. 'So yes, sure thing.'

'Sure thing what?' Laura demanded, 'What are you talking about?'

'Manners please Miss Clemence.' Mr McIntosh put his hands on his skinny hips. He was wearing khaki shorts, black formal dress shoes with white socks pulled up to just under his knee. Long socks seemed to be in vogue with all the male teachers at our school. 'Your uncle will be assisting me in directing the performances for the Agricultural Fair.'

'Uncle Melvin won't be able to go to the fair because livestock makes him ill. When we went last year he walked past the cow sheds and he nearly spewed and said the smell followed him around the grounds so he couldn't escape it and he nearly passed out in sideshow alley and a group of ladies laughed at him.'

'I had 'flu. Stop lying to your teacher!'

Laura was unfazed. 'We don't need any help with our dance, by the way. So you can help Toby Hawkins with his monologue or whatever he's doing.'

Toby Hawkins was the year seven thespian. He only got more intolerable as we entered high school. He would walk around handing fake red roses to all the girls and giving them compliments, the kind you find on cheap Valentine's Day lollies. The ones that taste like ash.

'Oh yes, Toby's Richard the Third? I am already in the process of sourcing him an underarm crutch and he's making a hunchback out of papier-mâché.' Melvin looked intensely pleased with his protégé. 'What have you two decided on then?'

'We're doing a dance to the music from *The Exorcist*,' Laura said.

'Typical,' said Melvin.

Mr MacIntosh was shocked. 'Oh good lord! Mel, who let them watch that?'

'I think it will be good.' I feebly interjected, wanting the interaction to end. 'Laura's really good at choreography.'

'Oh dear. Alberta if you are impressed you must both be planning some sort of Grand Guignol extravaganza.' Melvin pointed an accusatory finger at me. 'This one's got my Laura into forbidden cinema, Alistair. It's completely out of my hands.'

'She didn't get me into anything, we both have liked scary films. Always. We can watch whatever we want, Mr McIntosh, because we know it's not real.' Laura stamped her foot to punctuate.

'She claims to be able to identify the pretence, completely immune to violence,' Melvin sighed.

'She's started to talk like you, Mel,' said Mr McIntosh. 'Better watch your nonsense doesn't rub off on Nina.'

Over the period in which Laura and I were not in contact due to the incident by the creek, Melvin's girlfriend Jade became pregnant and she had recently given birth to a baby girl. When Laura and I met Nina (and Jade) Laura refused to hold Nina because she was scared she would drop her on her head like she had her cousin Corbin. Daddy Jonathan told Laura not to be ridiculous, that she knew perfectly well she'd never met her cousin Corbin, that he lived with her Aunt Lucy and Uncle Don in England. Laura argued the point with her father while I held Nina and sniffed her head. I usually liked the smell of baby heads, but this baby's head smelled like nothing. Usually a baby smells of something — vomit, shit, stewed vegetables — but Nina smelled like she had nothing inside. She smelled like air.

The Performing Arts Showcase at the Agricultural Fair was a yearly extracurricular activity for students of more artistic persuasions. Laura and I were in the middle of rehearsals one lunch break when Mother Ann arrived unannounced and told me that, when everyone else went back to class, I was to meet with a lady who was visiting to find out how I was coping being the sibling of a child 'like Louis'. I refused to go. Laura placed her palm lightly on my head as she always did when she could sense I was upset, and walked away. I ran away from Mother Ann and out to the car park, looking around frantically for her car, finding it increasingly difficult to breathe.

Mother Ann caught up with me and apologised for not telling me sooner. She thought I might perform better under pressure, not dwell on the impending occasion.

'It will be good for you to talk to someone. I can't go with you,' she said.

'Why not? I can't do anything by myself. I can't. And you've seen me try — I just can't.'

'June will be there.'

'I don't even know June and why does she need to be there? She has no right; it's none of her business.'

'She needs to hear about what Louis' home life is like.'

'None of her business!' I wailed again.

June Brontle was a bad-tempered, bitter beast of a woman who acted as Louis' aide in the Special Education Centre. Mother Ann was always accidentally calling her 'June Brontë', which makes me imagine June as the lost, uncultivated, illiterate Brontë sister; driven from her family's meagre homestead into the streets and forced to sell onions. My mother did tuckshop duty a few times a month and told me they always had to set aside the parson's nose for June when they were cutting up chicken to make sandwiches. June only ate meat. June was on a carbohydrate-free diet so she could only eat chook's arseholes.

I started to hyperventilate which turned into something part way between a cough and a choking sound, like my lungs were literally barking orders to my brain to stop trying to kill me. A pair of mothers who worked at the tuckshop were out on the footpath having a smoke break, listening to everything we said.

'Sounds like she just needs a good hard smack to me,' we heard one of them say.

'Bitch,' Mother Ann said, under her breath. She dragged me into the backseat of the car and slammed the door behind us. Her face was flushed with as much anger as mine was with sorrow. She instructed me as calmly as she could that if I could just sit out on the benches in the playground, in the fresh air with June and the psychologist and answer the questions it would make her very proud of me. She said she would wait for me around the corner, just out of sight, in case I needed help.

I sat on a cold bench next to June repeating the word 'bitch' over and over again in my head. June introduced the woman sitting opposite us, who was wearing a dress suit and had lines around her thin lips, much like one of those Galápagos tortoises that live forever. Her name was Catherine Wilkes and she was a child psychologist. It made me wonder whether she wasn't smart enough to be an adult psychologist. She pursed her reptilian lips and asked me how I was feeling.

'Bad, but not all the time so it's not important,' I said, peeling paint off the bench in long defiant strips.

'And why is that?'

'I shouldn't have to do this. I nearly fainted from not breathing.'

'And do you often have trouble breathing?'

'All the time. Can I go?'

'We'd just like to have a little chat,' said June.

'About why having a brother like mine is terrible?'

'You think it's terrible?' Catherine Wilkes looked hungry for drama.

'Am I supposed to pretend it's easy? Is that the polite thing to do?'

'Well we could start there. Your mother tells me you can get quite angry with your…is it Louis? Is that true?'

June Brontle nodded at her.

'Why? Is being angry not allowed?'

'It's certainly not the best way to be,' said June Brontle. Catherine Wilkes shook her head at her, as if to tell her that was the wrong thing to say.

I felt like everyone wanted to tell me how cruel I was, wanted to tell me how I was not allowed to feel in any way inconvenienced by Louis' behaviour, by the fact that he took up most of Mother Ann's time, like everything I said and felt was to do with him, it was like even my emotions belonged to him. He could hit me across the face and head-butt me and I had to take it and smile and help Mother Ann out but at the same time not get in the way. I began to cry again, this time in low incensed hiccups, the only thing stopping me from screaming obscenities at these women.

'Your mother says you spend an awful lot of time at your friend's house,' June Brontle said.

'Why is that?' asked Catherine Wilkes, who suggested I take a sip from my water bottle before continuing. I said I hated the smell of the plastic. That the air smelled disgusting too, and I wanted to go home. I tried to take a drink, but I felt like I couldn't swallow. I couldn't think. All I could do was spit the water out in a large porpoise-like spray all over Catherine Wilkes.

'Oh come now!' she screeched in a high-pitched whine that negated her veneer of professionalism.

I got dragged by June Brontle back to my mother who took me home, humiliated. I remember telling her on the way, after I'd stopped sobbing:

'I don't want to spend the rest of my life being dragged around by June.'

I couldn't bear the thought of my brother being constantly in the care of this absurd Dickensian cow. I was relieved when it turned out June Brontle was indeed the monster I considered her to be. Her abusive methods in the classroom were exposed by Louis himself. June Brontle's favourite method of disciplining her little 'spazzles', as she called them, was to sit on them until they stopped screaming. One day, Louis was locked in a supply closet for four hours and, being so desperate to piss, he had to do it in a box of coloured yarn.

'I did a wee in the wool,' he said in a frightened voice to Mother Ann one afternoon.

Mother Ann did some investigating and found that other students had come home with similar stories. She found Louis a place at a specialised school down the coast. He caught a taxi from outside the solicitor's office and returned on his first afternoon brighter, like an old man that had retired to the seaside and given himself over to the peace and the air. I wouldn't have to worry about Louis' presence at school any more. I selfishly believed this change was most beneficial to me, of course, because I was a bad sister and a bad daughter who spat on healthcare professionals.

19 / THE DEVIL MAY CARE BUT I DON'T MIND

Laura and I had devised a ludicrous dance number to 'Tubular Bells' by Mike Oldfield. Daddy Jonathan kept a cassette of it in his car and Laura nabbed it once she realised it was the music used in *The Exorcist*, which we had recently seen thanks to Hayley, who had dropped a bag of video tapes on Laura's doorstep and run away before anyone saw him. Judging by the quality of the tape, it appeared to be a copy of a copy of a copy, likely passed around at the high school, but that somehow made the film even more engrossing. The graininess, the pixilation that occurred in the scenes with very little light meant we constantly thought we were seeing things in the background that weren't really there. Poor colour depth meant that a translucent figure could be found in what was merely intended to be a pitch-black room.

'Tubular Bells' doesn't have the kind of beat you can dance to. We had such trouble trying to keep in step with the frenetic pace of the melody that Laura suggested we ignore it altogether and make it up as we went along, with just a few key elements, including me crouching on all fours and Laura draping herself over me to make it look like she was Regan levitating from her bed. We hoped on the day of the performance I could hold her up and she could keep her balance and not end up in an awkward heap as we had often done in rehearsals.

. . .

We found out on the day of the Agricultural Fair that we were to perform on the back of a large truck. Laura was not pleased. By association, her hatred of all truck drivers extended to their vehicles. There were bales of hay piled on the back of the flatbed of the truck to avoid performers falling backwards and onto the ground, but also, I suspect, this set up was designed to look quaint and rural.

'I hate it, I hate it, *I hate it*,' Laura moaned, as we got ready in a nearby toilet block. We both wore our black leotards with white night-dresses over the top. Our faces were painted a sickly light green, with haphazard red streaks to look like the cuts Regan makes on her face with the crucifix. Melvin had promised Mr MacIntosh that we wouldn't 'do anything too controversial', but something in the way Melvin had said this made me think he really wanted us to.

'Do we look possessed enough?' I asked as we gazed at ourselves in the dirty mirror of the public lavatory.

Laura sighed. 'It'll have to do.'

I put my arm around her shoulder. 'Are you still worried about the truck?'

She thought for a second. 'Nah, I'm fine.'

We stood at the bottom up the stairs leading up to the stage. I looked out at the audience and noticed very few people. I could see Mother Ann, chatting to our teacher. When Mr MacIntosh announced us (reluctantly) we entered the stage as though blown by a great gust of wind, throwing ourselves back and forth across the stage. I tried to match Laura's movements, or at least complement them. Instead of lying across my back as rehearsed, she straddled me like a horse reaching her arms to the heavens and convulsing as if channeling a demon. We must have looked ludicrous.

When 'Tubular Bells' started to fade out, as the pièce de résistance, we each reached for a small vial of green glitter which we proceeded to 'vomit' into the front row of the audience, most of whom were mean-dering toddlers. A young girl of no more than two was patting her tiny palms against the grass and lifted her hands to us to show off the glitter she had accumulated. Then I heard Laura scream and suddenly she was grabbing my arm and pulling me off the side of the truck. We ran – Laura pulling me through crowds lining up for sample bags and rides; the smell of fat and sugar lingering in the air as she hauled me, finally, behind a giant jumping castle. We sat in the shadow of the behemoth, a loud industrial hissing coming from the pump that was keeping the thing filled with air. The grating bass of bargain-basement techno music pumped desperately from a large speaker behind my head.

Laura was sobbing. The heaving, distressed kind of sob that was second nature to me but had never before seen manifest so violently in my friend. The only thing I could do was wait for her to stop. She didn't. I could tell she couldn't. I tried to touch her arm but she pulled it away, throwing herself face down onto the grass. I started crying too, my head aching from being too nervous to eat prior to the performance. The sickly, sideshow smells. The constant hissing of a giant inflatable in my ears. I remembered all the times I had hidden, trembling in confined spaces. I was simultaneously sad for her, resentful of her, and hurt she didn't want my comfort. I lay down next to her, placed my forehead against her temple that was contracting and sweating green face paint. This time she didn't recoil from me.

'It was him,' she sniffed. 'Didn't you see him too?'

I said I didn't.

She started sobbing again. She turned her back on me and started saying 'you don't believe me' over and over.

I tried to pull her into a sitting position and she cooperated reluctantly. She looked up at me. Her face paint had nearly completely rubbed off, replaced by dirt and tears. *I have been here before*, I thought.

All I could say to Laura was that I did believe her. And it was true, I did believe in Mister San Hosantio, but for some reason it only felt real when I saw him too and that was mostly in my dreams. I suggested maybe he appeared to us in different ways.

I waited for her breathing to slow. She wiped her face on her nightdress, leaving a green stain that made her Regan costume look even more authentic. Then I suggested we find Mother Ann to take us home. I led her by the hand back to the performance area.

'I should tell Hayley,' Laura said.

I wanted to ask her why, why did we need to include Hayley in everything when he didn't even care? Why did she think Hayley was going to be of any help at all? But I kept my mouth shut, because I knew what happened last time I stood up for myself.

As Mother Ann drove us home, Laura explained to her that she was upset because she had a stomach ache, and that the screaming — that was all part of the act. She knew that's the phrase adults like to hear, and they always believed her because Laura had always been the kind of girl to fall flat on her face and immediately jump up declaring: 'I meant to!' Her histrionics were for dramatic effect —she'd grow out of them soon enough.

I sat confused and nervous for hours after we dropped Laura off. Mother Ann had just grilled me about how I even knew anything about *The Exorcist*. That I had embarrassed her in front of Miss Miller and the other parents. I lied and said it was on TV and Laura and I were just up late watching when we shouldn't have been and I was very sorry and it was most certainly not Laura's fault. Mother Ann said she wasn't blaming Laura, especially considering how out of sorts she seemed after the performance. I tried to convince Mother Ann that seeing the film had not had a negative effect on us. She found that difficult to believe. She had seen it at the cinema with Father Robert when she was only nineteen and had gone to a Catholic school and implored me to imagine how terrible it would be for someone brought up to believe the devil actually exists.

The need to know Laura was okay, that she wasn't doing anything stupid, became so strong that I decided to call her. We had found a solution to my fear of making phone calls. If I needed to speak to Laura, I would call her, let the phone ring twice and hang up. Then she would call me back. I didn't have to say anything when I answered, she would just start talking. But even on the phone to my best friend, I felt a tension that was absent when we communicated face to face. I couldn't shake the low, almost animal voice of that prank caller: *Mr Howard, I love you*. I felt like this voice might one day intercept one of my telephone conversations with Laura and tell me something much more frightening. Laura's phone rang twice and I hung up. I got no call in response until the following morning.

'She still sounds sick,' said Mother Ann, surprised, before handing me the receiver.

Laura did seem hoarse.

'So — I called Hayley, and Bill answered. I thought for a minute he would hang up on me but he didn't. Hayley seemed annoyed, but I just wanted to know, to find out, you know, if Helen sees shadow men too? I mean she said she did and that her mum saw the full-on ghost of her Aunty Vera so I thought maybe...I don't really know what I'm doing.'

'Do you want me to come over?' I asked.

'No. I'll deal with it,' she said before hanging up.

20 / 'COULD YOU HELP AN OLD ALTER BOY, FATHER?'

Most school holidays, Mother Ann would drive us to the city and leave Louis and I to visit with our father for a few days. Louis would start crying for her almost as soon as she left and Father Robert would shut himself in his bedroom, leaving me to fumble through a large duffle bag full of Louis' favourite videos, desperate to find one that would placate him.

On this particular visit, however, Louis was strangely calm. He sat transfixed by the TV and Father Robert made me a cup of tea with lots of sugar and tried to ask me normal questions like how did I feel about starting high school? Did I know what I wanted to do with my life? It felt like he was rushing through years of what he assumed to be common questions to ask a young girl, getting the timeline confused (was I in grade seven or eight now?). Forcing what he considered to be a natural father/daughter dialogue, getting it all out of the way so he didn't have to bother with it later. He asked me if I had received my thirteenth birthday present (a small ceramic ornament of a Golden Retriever listening to a Walkman) and I said yes thank you very much and changed the subject quickly because — even though I had no reason to believe so — if we continued talking about my age he might say something gross like Pa.

When staying with Father Robert, I usually slept on a lumpy fold-out cot in his spare room, Louis on an inflatable mattress beside me. I couldn't sleep so I got out of bed to get a glass of water. Father Robert was sitting in his peeling brown leather chair in front of the television and when I looked at the screen I was confronted by the image of a little girl in a pretty white dress cuddling and scratching the belly of a big fat cane toad like it was a puppy. I backed away in revulsion and terror. Father Robert laughed without remorse and sent me back to bed with my water before whispering through a crack in the door:

'You know I heard on the radio the other day that toads are getting bigger. One day they'll be the size of a horse.'

When Mother Ann came to collect us, I told her what had happened. The incident with Pa had made her more affectionate towards me. She stroked my back and promised a toad could never make it inside the house. I started raving on about how you can tell toads are evil because they look like a deflated rubber ball that has been set on fire and they had the furious face of a vengeful old man, that they weren't even supposed to be here, that if another animal tried to eat one it would die and how could Mother Ann be sure one couldn't get inside? We'd only have to leave the door open for a second for one to hop on in and then what would we do? I told them that I often lay awake in the night imagining a toad-like nightmare machine — half metal and half flesh — that walked through the world projecting my hurt onto others, making their lives unbearable and once I shut down for the night the world heaved a collective sigh and experienced what is universally recognised as 'happiness'.

'And you think I'm a lunatic,' Father Robert said to Mother Ann.

I thought – at times – I might be the source of everyone's sorrow. It's part of the sickness that makes you turn in on yourself until you can't imagine there would be anyone else to blame. Not even when Laura told me about the scratching in her chest or I looked into Helen's glassy sedated eyes — that was me. If I were somehow healed, everyone else's problems would be solved. I wanted to ask Father Robert if his sickness began with me. Instead I said:

'Mother Ann and Valerie had a talk and now they've forced me and Laura to get the bus to school.'

Father Robert winced. He knew I had been fighting it for years. Mother Ann told him I had to gain some independence 'before it was too late.' Meaning, she wanted me to make like a good girl and piss off out of home as soon as I finished school.

'It's so loud sometimes I have to stick my fingers in my ears,' I told Father Robert of the bus. 'Grade ones sit in the front, twelves in the back. We sit kind of in the middle. It's awful. It's cramped and it smells.'

'Thirteen-year-old boys have the worst B.O.' Father Robert added.

'What have boys got to do with Bob and Oona?' I thought he was talking about some boisterous friends of Uncle Lyle's who took Mother Ann and him on a disastrous windsurfing trip in 1976. 'Look at those awful B.O.s' he would say when he spotted some people on television he didn't like.

'A stranger looks at your father sideways and they've got an enemy for life. One they'll never know exists,' Mother Ann said of Father Robert's irrational grudges.

It made me think about all the little things that stop me from sleeping. A glance, a word, a detailed nocturnal analysis that turns the smallest of incidents into a traumatic event, making it hard to completely forgive anyone.

Getting the bus was even more difficult when Laura wasn't with me. Once, Valerie called at me from over the fence and said that Laura was sick and wouldn't be going to school. I went back inside and told Mother Ann I was ill as well. She didn't believe me. She asked in an exasperated tone why I couldn't do things alone 'like all the other kids'. Being a perpetual cop-out was easier than facing the crush of bodies alone.

The bus collected each student individually from outside their homes, so Laura and I would wait on the footpath outside my front gate, waiting for the rattling old beast to push its way down the narrow road. When we couldn't sit together we would stand in the aisle. Mrs Sampson, the bus driver — a tense, quiet woman — wasn't one for discipline. And Laura's verbal dysentery was a welcome distraction from all the other voices shrieking and moaning over one another. Luckily I could still hear Laura even if she were whispering to me across an airport tarmac.

. . .

I understood – well before I received any psychiatric assistance – that all doctors have their own brand of manipulation. I had a displaced eye tooth, one that had grown down from the top of my gum. If I pulled my lip up, it looked like a vampire's fang, the kind that would grow before feasting on blood and retract afterwards. The fang, combined with my split uvula, made my mouth a concealed cabinet of curiosities. It didn't matter that no one could see inside, the fact that I was aware of it was enough.

Mother Ann took me to the dentist. He was awful, not because of the camp Transylvanian accent he employed when examining my fang, but because he suggested Mother Ann pay for me to get braces she couldn't afford because I was 'such a pretty girl' and I 'wouldn't want to ruin it all by having gnarly teeth,' would I? Laura was incensed when I told her. She wondered why he couldn't just yank it out, as it was nowhere near my other teeth, so how could this wayward fang actually misalign them? Laura said the dentist just wanted more money to fund his new luxury yacht, his racehorse and his secret wife in Santorini.

Wanting a second opinion, Mother Ann took me to another dentist (to my relief, a female this time), who said I didn't need braces and all I needed to fix the problem was to do exactly as Laura had suggested. I was anaesthetised, but she had to tug the tooth quite hard to dislodge it and for a few weeks it left a gaping wound where the tooth used to be.

'Look at my big red hole,' I said to Laura, lifting my upper lip.

'That's a gross way to put it. I think I'm going to miss that fang,' she said.

I wondered where the wayward tooth in my brain was, and could it also be removed? Was there a kind of worm, a parasite in there that, with precision and care, could be extracted in order to make me functional, rational? Perhaps I would be able to confidently board a bus if I just scratched away at my body, plucked hairs from my head, peeled away some skin, performed some ritual of self-mutilation, and turned myself inside out. Vanish.

21 / 'HAVE YOU EVER BOUGHT OR RENTED A VIDEO CASSETTE THAT WASN'T QUITE RIGHT?'

My first year of high school started poorly. Mother Ann couldn't pull the strings anymore, so Laura and I ended up in different classes. My English teacher, Mrs Wells, picked on me all the time because I was too quiet and whenever she asked me a question I would give her a 'disrespectful, dirty look', as she wrote on my mid-year report card. I knew that when I was confused, I would screw my face up a little. Laura called it the 'Albert Special', which she described to me as a scowl and pout in one. It made it easy for her to tell when I was uncomfortable. But I don't believe I stared Mrs Wells down in a bid to annihilate her, as she seemed to believe.

Rachael Gold sat next to me in these classes. We never said much to each other, but we had some unspoken agreement that when the room was full of louder, more unsavoury students (Our class, 8-L, earned the reputation amongst the teachers as the worst juniors they'd ever had, dubbing us 'Eight Hell') that we would pair up for protection.

Laura spent her time away from me listening and observing. She wasn't outspoken in class either, but she kept her head up, could look people in the eye, and she listened. And learned. She would regale me with tales of girls in her home class who had already had sex, smoked weed, wore perfume, had their belly buttons pierced and other things that we were supposed to suddenly be interested in now we were teenagers. Laura said one girl asked her if Hayley was in a band and seemed heartbroken when Laura told her no, that just because a boy has long hair and wears flannel shirts doesn't make him a musician by default.

'I told her he works at the fruit shop in the afternoons, then goes home and sulks. I really have no idea what the big deal is,' she said.

I assumed, though I didn't tell her so, that Laura was stretching the truth about how often we had contact with Hayley. We recently learned he had a girlfriend named Hannah Francis, a girl not of the same disordered, eccentric variety as Laura or me. She was a carefully constructed entity, the kind we were taught boys preferred: blonde streaks in her hair, short skirts, she even wore eyeliner to school much to Laura's chagrin as she was considering wearing eyeliner too at some point but now she couldn't because people would talk. She didn't want anyone to think she wanted to be like Hannah, or that she gave two tosses about Hayley.

We would sometimes watch them, from a safe distance. Hayley fidgeting and looking away, Hannah desperately trying to make conversation.

'Does he ever talk?' I asked.

'Probably not. But why is Hannah even bothering? He's grotty, he's always been grotty, since when was grotty cool? If I never washed my hair and walked around with clothes with holes in them I doubt any boys would be lining up to date me or ask if I was in a grotty band.'

'Can you say "grotty" again?' I asked.

Laura threw a piece of mandarin skin at my head.

I barely flinched. She threw another. I didn't even blink.

'Wow, you're almost brave, Al.'

I could appreciate that Laura had really doubled down on the Hayley scorn after what happened by the creek. But it seemed performative. She badmouthed him constantly and I pretended to be oblivious to the extent that I started shielding my eyes from him as he went by, like Valerie did with Laura.

Sometimes Laura would justify her fixation on Hayley's personal life by talking of how much she wanted to see Helen again. She wanted to know how the story of her mother, Agnes, ended, whether she was right about Ed Monterey being a relation, if the ghost of her Aunt Vera appeared to her and in what capacity. She had not mentioned Mister San Hosantio once since the Agricultural Fair –

almost a year ago. When she said she would 'deal with it' the tone of her voice implied that the name was now somehow cursed and that maybe if we never spoke it, neither of us would see him again. I couldn't tell her about my dreams anymore. I didn't feel like I was supposed to, because we had to grow up.

Laura had been asking her father to buy her a double bed. Valerie opposed the idea, saying that Laura had no need for one until she was an adult, that being thirteen was not akin to maturity. They had argued so much about it Laura was punished by being given the task of defrosting and wiping down the fridge. Laura hated the scent of vanilla, and Valerie used a homemade concoction of methylated spirits and vanilla essence to clean the entire kitchen. She was in the middle of a sneezing fit when Valerie led me into the kitchen, giving me strict instructions not to help her, that she needed to learn to cease her relentless attempts to drive her father to a nervous breakdown. Valerie gestured for me to look out the kitchen window at Jonathan, lying immobile on a sun lounge in the middle of the yard, a brown cable-knit cardigan over his face. I was always apprehensive about what I would see outside that window. I was surprised Laura wasn't more wary of it after what she saw the day she moved in, but I couldn't ask her, because we had to be teenagers now, and with that came rationality. Laura tossed a vanilla-soaked rag into the sink and watched her father. She sniffed and rubbed at her nose. Valerie and I stood behind her and we all looked out at this prostrate man far longer than was necessary, as though waiting for a sign, the merest echo of mortality.

'You're finished now. Go.' said Valerie holding her hand to her face as Laura pushed past her and thudded up the stairs. I heard a door slam. Valerie dropped her hand and turned to me.

'Didn't I say you could go?'

I started up the stairs, stomping my feet as well because I wanted to know what it felt like. I heard the shower running. Laura was scrubbing away the scent. I went into her bedroom. All the covers had been stripped from her bed and lay neatly arranged in the same manner on the floor, surrounded by clothes, wet towels, a cassette labelled merely 'songs' in lead pencil with all the tape ripped out.

Compared to Laura's room, the rest of the Clemence house was spotless. There was no clutter, not even the slightest bit of dust on the skirting boards. Laura's room remained in disarray because Valerie reasoned that Laura should learn to clean up her own mess. Really, it was because she didn't want the kind of intimacy of picking up dirty underwear that belonged to a girl she couldn't even look in the face. I lay down on the floor-bed and studied the knotted pine ceiling. It was like having hundreds of distorted alien faces staring down at me. I focused my attention on one with giant twisted spiralling eyes, a disproportionately small dot for a nose and the slightest crescent fingernail for a mouth.

Laura tore back into the room with an enormous beach towel covered in hibiscus flowers wound at least twice around her torso. She asked me if I liked her new bed as she rummaged through her wardrobe huffing and hawing about not being able to find any clean clothes before collapsing next to me in an oversized grey marle t-shirt. She explained that the reasons she had decided to vacate her bed were twofold: it was both a protest against Daddy Jonathan's refusal to buy her a double bed and a desire to know what it felt like to have a larger sleeping space. A 'bed without edges'.

'Because you know how I'm always falling out?' she asked.

Frequently, when I spent the night on a foam mattress next to Laura's bed she would make me believe she had fallen asleep. Then, after vocalising a certain amount of comedic peril ('woah-oh-oh no!') she would fall hard, often right on top of me, then pretend to be shocked and distressed in an attempt to convince me that the manoeuvre was completely spontaneous, that her body acted before her mind, that it was like sleepwalking, that she only woke up once she had winded me and almost broken my ribs.

'Yes, that sure is a problem,' I said with overt sarcasm. 'Does that mean I get to sleep in your bed from now on?'

Laura frowned, like she was concerned about giving me that kind of privilege. She said no. That I was to sleep next to her on the mattress I always used. However, she would lie on the carpet, because it would probably hurt her back and then Jonathan — she'd recently dropped the 'Daddy' and adopted the habit of obstinate, worldly teenagers in films who wish to undermine their parents by calling them by their first name — would have to buy her a double bed.

'I'm trying it for the first time tonight. Are you going to stay?'

I said I would like to as I wanted to talk to her about what had been happening at school because after telling Mother Ann about the way Mrs Wells was treating me, she had organised to meet with her to discuss the teacher's inexplicable vendetta — that had come to a head when she'd asked me to answer a question about adverbs and when I said I didn't know the answer, she repeated what I said back to me in an embellished melancholy tone.

'She used the duh voice,' I explained to Laura, 'And when Mother Ann asked her why she did it Mrs Wells said it never happened.'

'Why didn't you tell me this?' Laura demanded.

'It just happened yesterday. I didn't get a chance and you were worried about Hannah Francis giving you that death stare in the tuck-shop line.'

'Ugh you know what?' Laura thought for a moment, as though she was ready to go off on another tirade about Hayley's girlfriend yet thought better of it and urged me to continue.

'Well, next week, Mrs Wells is either going to be super nice to me or extra awful. Mother Ann said she felt intimidated into agreeing that I was making it all up and she just told her I would be more considerate or something from now on.'

I sniffed away some tears and Laura sat up and began dabbing at my face with the hem of her t-shirt. It smelled like man. It was definitely one of Jonathan's cast offs. I lightly pushed her away.

'You should never let your parents get involved,' said Laura. I assumed that was the lie she told herself in order to justify her father's lack of interest. In the moment, though, it heightened my paranoia. Laura suggested that Mother Ann ask that I change to another class. I said she'd tried, and the teacher in charge of the department — who was clearly a friend of Mrs Wells —told Mother Ann she couldn't give me 'special treatment', that if any other students found out it was possible to change classes she would have an insurgence of disenfran-chised youths of her hands. Laura said that meant the head of department believed every teacher in the school (granted there weren't many) was an absolute monster, which was probably true. Her English teacher, Mr Darren, was fresh out of university and let them watch films instead of read books.

'Last week he brought his video camera in to film our presentations and he only turned it on when it was a girl's turn. Not every girl, just a few of them. I could tell because Jonathan has that same camcorder and the light always flashes green when it's filming. I was sitting right next to the tripod for the entire lesson and I know who he filmed and who he didn't.'

'Did he film you?' I asked.

'No,' she said, 'and I'm not sure if it's because he didn't want to or because he knew I was on to him.'

'You should tell someone, though.'

'Who would believe me?'

I nodded in agreement and began to cry again. Laura assured me (in a slightly impatient manner) that it would all be okay and that Valerie had promised to drive us to the video store if Laura successfully cleaned the fridge, which she was sure she did because even after showering, she could still smell vanilla and would I please check to see if she was correct in feeling a rash developing on the back of her thighs. She wasn't.

We were having a covert meeting in the back corner of the video store, next to the horror films and the soft-core pornography. Laura was furious that a new policy had been introduced which involved new release tapes (the six-dollar, overnight rentals) being kept behind the counter and only placed in the case after confirmation of purchase. I told Laura she would just have to wait until *Interview with the Vampire* became a weekly rental as I crouched behind her swapping *Little Women* out for a copy of *An American Werewolf in London*. We'd been doing this for quite a while. It was my idea. The owner of the store, Hayley's friend Barry, never checked the inside of the case unless someone claimed the tape was damaged. We had to rewind every video we rented before we watched it because no one heeded Barry's sign, a piece of yellowing cardboard tacked up by the door that read 'Remember to rewind' next to which he had drawn a banana wearing sunglasses. Both Laura and I were tempted to ask Barry what possessed him to draw the banana —what relevance it had to rewinding video cassettes or films in general — but Barry was intimidating. Not in the way you would usually describe a surly man in his thirties. He was, at a guess, over six feet tall and incredibly thin. He had small, pale eyes, a waxy face and ginger hair that he kept in a short, square buzz cut. He never smiled and when he served us he would bend over the counter like a straw to take our money. This is what made the drawing of the banana even more baffling — the man seemed devoid of enthusiasm, or, at the very least, the kind of oddball humour that would compel one to even conceive of an anthropomorphic piece of fruit.

The intimidating nature of Video Store Barry also meant that we were both afraid of bringing to his attention any faults in the tapes. Jonathan had recently let Laura wheel his television into her room for what was supposed to be one night only but it ended up as a permanent fixture after he had (apparently) decided after reading a locally-published 'alternative news' publication that the radiation emitted from the cathode ray was much stronger and more dangerous than we realised. When I asked Laura why, if he believed such a thing, would Jonathan put her in danger of radiation poisoning, she merely responded:

'It's supposed to kill sperm so I'm immune.'

The VCR did not like *An American Werewolf in London*. It kept ejecting the tape as soon as we pushed it in.

'Don't like the taste of this one, do you?' Laura mumbled to herself and she pushed the tape back in, harder and harder each time until I told her she would damage the machine if she kept on.

She moved aside, frustrated. I lifted up the back panel of the cassette to see if there was any damage to the tape itself. Having to constantly repair our VCR after the abuse it suffered at the hands of Louis had made me quite adept at identifying common playback issues. I turned the reels around a few times to make sure the tape wasn't chewed up. It looked fine. Laura asked me whether I needed to take the top off the machine because she wouldn't have the faintest idea where to find a screwdriver. After a few more attempts the tape stayed in long enough for us to see about three seconds of static over the Village Roadshow logo before it ejected again. Laura threw her pillow at the television unit. She said we needed to find someone to help us. That she would take the tape to school and ask Hayley to look at it. She reasoned that because he was friends with Barry he may have learned something about how videos work. I told her fine, as long as I didn't have to be there when it happened.

Laura pretended to sleep well that night. When we settled down at about 1am she insisted we keep the television running, playing reams of music videos on low volume. I lay awake thinking about Mrs Well's impending revenge, and how badly Hayley would react to Laura's request to see what was wrong with the videotape. Reliving every uncomfortable memory I ever had over and over. I tried to focus my attention on the screen, on what Laura would call 'grotty men' stomping about an industrial wasteland; women dressed as dolls, clean-cut British men flailing about a council estate, a redheaded woman playing the piano, a short, feeble-looking man levitating in slow motion. Each time I attempted to turn the television off Laura would swat my hand away mumbling: 'No, no, is good song, stoppit go sleep.'

I looked down at her, curled up in a foetal position on top of her sheets, in front of the TV unit, likely finding some comfort in the low hum of the music but not — as I was — disturbed by the intrusive light from the screen. We had decided to sleep in a t-shape, just because. I sat up. I felt like I was reclining on a dais, like I was the master and she was the servant. At around 3am, when I was sure she was asleep, I successfully switched the television off. A Nine Inch Nails video — not intended to be viewed by someone with epilepsy — was making me nauseous. I lay on my back in the dark, still seeing irregular shapes flickering on the ceiling. A floater that looked like bacteria under a microscope hovered around in front of my eyes; I closed them and repeated the word 'nothing' over and over in my head, hoping that those crippling thoughts would not return and allow me at least a few hours of peace. But what if I — nothing. What if I never — nothing, nothing, nothing.

I heard a rumbling outside, getting closer. The sound of car tyres skidding around the corner and roaring past, the headlights on high-beam illuminating the window. As the sound of the engine disap-peared into the distance, the light in the window remained. It looked like there was a streetlight shining through the curtains, like I was used to seeing when I slept over at Father Robert's. I was hoping it was another illusion, some residue. I tried opening my eyes and closing them again, putting the covers over my head for a minute or so — but the light remained. Laura was curled in an awkward position. Her arms were straight, as though they were tied to her knees, like the sacrificial lamb in that old Baroque painting. It looked like she wasn't breathing. It felt like we had both died and I, alone, had been resurrected. I considered whether, when I was not with Laura, she stayed like this, only to be revived when I needed her.

I pulled the curtain aside. In the minimal moonlight, I could just make out the shape of the tall trees that obscured the view of my house. I closed the curtains. The light returned. I opened them again to darkness. I heard a crackling in the bougainvillea below the window. Another car approached, slowly this time, but something about the sound of the engine, the rough, guttural hum, made me believe it was the same one. It knew I was watching and turned around. I was being surveyed. I ducked down below the window and listened. I heard the car idle for a brief moment right outside before speeding off again. The light in the window was gone. I felt my way back to my mattress. I heard a dog bark. Then the cane toads started rattling and I lay there, tense and sweating under a blanket that was far too thick. Had the toads been rattling the whole time? Had I only just noticed them, or had they started only at the height of my fear?

When I woke up, it was 11am. I could hear Laura downstairs, shouting at Janus. I got into the shower, sat down and closed my eyes as the cool water ran over my head. I must have sat there in a prolonged daze because Laura started knocking at the door. When I turned the water off she yelled through the door:

'Hurry up, I found a snake.'

It wasn't a real snake. I wouldn't exit the bathroom until Laura swore it wasn't. It was a rubber, red-bellied black.

'His name is Cyril,' Laura said, draping him around my neck. Laura pointed out the flakes of dried glue just below Cyril's head. When he was a child, Jonathan had glued it back on after Melvin was compelled to cut it off with a kitchen knife. I said I couldn't imagine Jonathan as one for practical jokes. It sounded more like Melvin's style

— he must have been one for japes. Laura agreed, but Jonathan had lived to torment his younger brother.

'Uncle Mel says that because Jonathan has always been so blasé about everything, it made being picked on really creepy. Of course, Mel would scream and scream and carry on like a dickhead but Jonathan would just walk away without ever saying sorry. He wouldn't even laugh.'

She took Cyril from around my neck and tossed him into the middle of the hall, for Valerie to find. Laura then explained to me that she had been awake since 8am and that she had thought through her idea about asking Hayley about the broken video and decided it wasn't worth pursuing. She asked me if we should just toss it out the window just to watch it break on the paving below. I thought for a moment before whispering:

'Yeah, go on.'

The cassette didn't break apart as we predicted, but it did end up with a large crack, right through the middle. I placed it back into the *Little Women* case. I told Laura I kind of felt sorry for the person who rented it next. She pointed out that the fact that Barry never inspected the tapes before re-shelving them wasn't our fault.

'After last night we can pretty much say that the thing was stuffed to begin with. You have to be prepared for that when you do business with Barry.' She rubbed her lower back.

'Little broken women,' I said.

The idea Laura lodged in my head — that Mrs Wells would become even more hostile after Mother Ann spoke to her — proved to be false. Instead of taunting me further, Mrs Wells just pretended I didn't exist. She didn't even look at me. It was like Valerie and Laura's relationship minus the concealed affection. On my report card, she gave me a B+ for English and refrained from adding anything in the box labelled 'comments'. Mr Darren, the camcorder pervert, wrote on Laura's report card that she was very observant but was lacking enthusiasm and charm. Like he was judging the Miss World pageant. C+

Now that we were in year nine, we could make sure we took all the same electives. I asked Laura if she thought being in the same class would distract us from our schoolwork. She said nonsense, bullshit, garbage — we concentrated better when we were together. She would frequently drift off into one of her reveries. When I managed to talk loud enough and long enough to bring her back, she would issue a barrage of apologies. She was starting to sound a lot like me. That wasn't to say the spontaneous, gregarious, dare I say 'effervescent' Laura was lost, she just showed up a little less. And I liked it.

During lunch, Laura and I would bunk down in the corner of the library and flip through old encyclopaedias about art, mythology, cryptozoology and the supernatural. Enormous tomes that could easily stun, if not kill, an intruder if you happened to have a copy by your bedside. Laura pointed out that it would be much more effective than Jonathan's bamboo stick, and did I know that when our parents were young, salespeople used to walk around the neighbourhood selling encyclopaedias? I asked her how they managed to carry a whole set from door to door. She said they were desperate for money and when you're desperate you can lift anything.

We were looking at William Blake's painting, 'The Night of Enitharmon's Joy'. Hecate, the underworld goddess with her three facets in front, a woman in black, despondent, her hand resting on an open book. Behind her, two naked figures kneel, hiding their faces. The book didn't give us any indication as to the significance of the group of strange creatures in the painting: a goofy-looking donkey, a comically startled owl and a bat-like creature with the face of a mustachioed deviant.

'They kind of ruin the whole thing, don't you think?' Laura asked. It's too much; they look like Muppets.'

'I sometimes feel like I'm three people,' I said, with little consideration, hoping Laura wasn't going to ask me what I meant.

Laura traced the curves of the image with her index finger. She pointed to the figure in the front. 'She's tired. Because the two naked people behind her, they're hiding their faces, they're there but they're not. She's carrying them and she's tired.'

'She wants to get rid of them?' I asked. 'It looks like they're hiding behind her and they're not complete humans yet because —'

'— who cares?' Laura quickly turned the page as though unnerved by the level of introspection we were attempting. 'Jesus, what was it with these guys and owls?' she asked, a sad chuckle, pointing to Goya's 'The Sleep of Reason Produces Monsters'.

Hayley appeared, unenthused, from behind a row of shelves.

'Yes?' Laura asked, feigning nonchalance.

'What?' I added, slamming the book shut on Laura's hand, which she immediately pulled out and used to smack me on the thigh.

'Mum wants to give you some old clothes,' Hayley said, addressing the floor.

'Um, which one of us are you talking to?' I asked.

'Who cares? Just come over on Saturday afternoon. She's usually awake by three, but don't come any later than four.' He slouched off without another word.

'He's going to cry,' said Laura with a curious tilt of the head.

I thought it was strange that Helen would ask for us after so long. Laura suggested we make her a present. She said it was important we make Helen happy, that Hayley would never have asked us to go and see her if he didn't think she really needed us and scoffed at my suggestion that because I'd been so quiet on our last visit, it was only Laura she wanted to see.

'She met you first, remember?'

'But I don't think she remembers she met me first,' I said.

'Don't be stupid,' Laura said, 'she doesn't have dementia, she knows perfectly well who we are.'

I was mystified, then, when Laura decided to crochet a blanket. 'Something for her to put on her lap when she's feeling bad,' was how she put it. When she actually sat down to begin the project, she had very little time left and became so overwhelmed she had to ask Valerie to do most of the work.

'I don't even like crochet, I don't know what I was thinking,' Laura said as we watched Valerie's hands finish off the last couple of stitches.

'That's what I'm here for. To do the thinking for you,' said Valerie.

I told Laura at least she had contributed to the gift. I was wondering how I could share the credit. Laura reminded me that I had picked the colours (purple and green) and the pattern (chevrons). However, it was too late for me to change my mind once I saw how garish the colours looked side-by-side. I knew Laura thought so too, but she also knew I would be distraught if she said so.

Valerie tossed the finished blanket at us with an almost disgusted finality and promptly left the room. Laura held it up in front of her face for my approval. 'You don't think it's too, you know, old lady?'

I lied and said no. The thing was archaic. Helen was only in her forties, I guessed. You give someone a crocheted blanket when you expect them to power down, to expire. My maternal great grand-mother had one on her lap the last time I saw her. Ma and Mother Ann had brought her some flowers and a teddy bear, which she hugged and sang to like it was a baby. 'Daisy' — that was the song she was singing —just like the computer, HAL, from *2001, A Space Odyssey*.

I called Laura and feigned illness on the day we were to deliver the horrible thing. She was audibly frustrated but didn't argue. I didn't want to experience the embarrassment of seeing the look of perplexity and feigned gratitude on Helen's face. But, then again, maybe Helen would love it. Maybe Hayley would love Laura for bringing the spark back into his mother's life through such a humble gesture. Maybe that was what Laura wanted. To have him and discard me. But I imagined Laura taking extreme liberties much more than she actually did. She had a bit more social clout than me, and sometimes said the wrong thing on impulse, but she would never deliberately hurt me.

I spent the day sulking about the house, slamming doors. When Mother Ann went outside to do some gardening, I grabbed a handful of cutlery out of the kitchen drawer and threw it onto the floor. I tried to break a plate, but the subtle buoyancy of the cork tiles left it lying there, intact. I wasn't getting the catharsis I expected from breaking things.

The way I was responding to the whole situation indicated a girl who had no comprehension of reality, had no idea of the appropriate response to pain and uncertainty. I might be able to see things with more clarity in retrospect, but when I was — am — enmeshed in The Dreadful Moment, I can't see anything but the knife. In this instance it was the literal paring knife that I (unhappy that the plate had survived its fall) threw point-first into the floor. It pierced the cork with a dull thud. Louis — suddenly able to hear the commotion over the sound of the television and his own piercing, relentless chatter — crawled up on top of the kitchen bench and peered down at my mess. Not his, for once. My mess.

'Mummy, mummy, blood and cut! Blood and cut!' he shouted until Mother Ann stumbled inside, cheeks pink, dirt on her hands swearing under her breath. Even when I explained to her there was no blood, that I'd been stupid and I was sorry, Louis continued to shout: 'Blood and cut!'

The biggest difference between Louis and me is that when I see a knife, Louis sees the knife too, but he also sees the blood.

Laura was late for class. She shuffled in, out of breath and sat at the end of the row of desks. Once she was settled, she leaned across Rachael who sat between us and started gesticulating and mouthing something I couldn't comprehend. Soon, Rachael passed me a note (folded in half too many times) that read: *Are you feeling okay???* She must have believed I was genuinely sick, a further indication that I had no idea how to read people. I saw Laura lean forward several times out of the corner of my eye, looking for a response to the point where Rachael risked being caught talking during silent reading time to ask me whether we needed to swap places. I shook my head. I didn't know what to write back. I couldn't do anything but sit with my guilt.

As soon as we were dismissed for lunch, Laura asked me again if I was okay. I said I wasn't sure, that it had been a weird couple of days. When I asked her about Helen, Laura thought for a moment before letting out an exaggerated sigh. We were lying on a steep hill that over-looked the tennis courts that no one ever used — not for tennis, anyway. The concrete was cracking, the lines were fading. One side of the court was blocked off by a concrete wall and we sometimes saw couples ineptly groping and fondling where they thought they couldn't be seen. It was Laura's opinion that they knew we could see, they just didn't care. Neither of us could understand why some people were proud of their inane teenage dry-humping. I found it difficult (and quite mortifying) to imagine anyone doing such a thing, let alone myself. I never directly brought up my indifference to sex with Laura as I wanted to believe she felt the same way as me about all things, but from the way she watched those bodies on the tennis court, when I would turn away — the words she used — told me it would be best just to ignore the topic altogether.

Laura said she had talked to Helen as much as she could in the hour she was allotted before Bill was due to burst through the door.

'Did you know Hayley bought a car? He's learning to drive. He takes it up the paddock. Knocked down part of the fence, doesn't give a shit if the Montereys notice.'

'I know, it's Pa's old ute.'

'Gross. He just gave it to him for free?'

I nodded. Laura said it was no wonder I hadn't told her. Was she acknowledging the fact that I didn't like talking about Pa or did she think I was deliberately withholding information? She made a point of saying that when she arrived at the Durstons, Hayley had pushed past her violently on his way out the door. She shoved her shoulder hard against mine to demonstrate.

'There was, you know, enough room for both of us in the doorway. He didn't have to go that far. Then Helen tells me he's going to drop out of school. He hasn't even finished year eleven and he's quitting.'

I knew this too. 'He's probably just going to work for Pa forever. Mother Ann said he's getting full-time work now.' It wasn't in our place to condemn Hayley's choices; neither of us were particularly ambitious.

Laura groaned.

'Imagine doing that for the rest of your life — hauling crates of pineapples around —'

'—driving a beige ute.'

'Fucking hell,' Laura said under her breath, pulling out grass by the fistful.

'But,' I asked, 'is Helen okay?'

Laura began rummaging through her backpack and pulled out the compact Nikon camera Jonathan had recently given to her. She began lazily snapping pictures of the sky then leant into me and turned the camera around. I cringed and protested. Laura said that I was making it worse for myself, that when she got the film developed, every single picture of me was going to be terrible precisely because I protested so much, that my face would be captured midway through whining 'no' or 'don't' or 'stop it' which was not very flattering and, honestly, incredibly tiresome.

I covered my face with my hands. 'No one wants to see my face, anyway.'

'Well get used to it because I'm going to be a photographer.'

'Since when?'

'Helen told me I should.'

'Okay but is she —'

'Okay? Yes. I think. She let me take some pictures of her. Is that a good sign?'

I said it probably was.

When Laura got the roll of film developed there were four or five photos of Helen sitting upright, the blanket draped over the back of the sofa. I could see it in her face that she was ready to break under the strain of being awake and amicable. But she did look, comparatively, 'okay'. In the background of one of the pictures I saw Hayley, slightly blurred, mid-stride. On his way out the door, I assumed.

I could tell Laura was at least attempting to treat photography as a potential vocation when she bought her first roll of black and white film. She spread the prints proudly across the dining table for her family and me to see. There was Rachael, sitting at a desk by a window, bright light streaming across her face. Jessie Benson, leaning her elbows against a chain-wire fence, the sleeves of her school uniform rolled up to her shoulders, the buttons undone revealing a piece of black leather cord around her neck.

Melvin tapped at it with enthusiasm.

'I know this one. A firebrand with a heart of gold.'

'What a stupid thing to say,' Jonathan mumbled, picking the photo up for closer inspection.

Jessie's mother worked at Melvin's health food store. Jessie and Laura now got along well, thanks, in part, to Rachael, who had invited us to a sleepover for her fifteenth birthday. We all slept in tents in Rachael's backyard and Jessie smuggled in a plastic bottle full of red wine she had taken from a cask in her mother's fridge and seeing as the only other guests willing to partake were Laura and me, we ended up a weeping, tipsy mess that ended with Jessie imploring Laura to slap her again because she deserved it. Laura had hugged her and said that no, no, she was the one who was in fact terrible and deserved to be hit twice, once for Jessie and once for walking away after Hayley punched me. As she said this, she stared at me over Jessie's heaving shoulders; the dark rings around her eyes accentuated by the light of the campfire.

'Hayley Durston punched you?' Rachael asked, sober and bewildered. I couldn't tell if she was angry or impressed.

'Not very hard,' I replied, staring back into Laura's eyes.

I had asked Laura not to choose any photographs of me to present to her family. When Valerie asked why there weren't any, I just told her I didn't like having my photo taken.

She said she could relate. 'You know, I don't think any photos of me exist after nineteen seventy-seven.'

When we were alone in her room, Laura produced the remaining photographs from her desk drawer.

'You're a screaming blur in quite a few,' she said, shuffling the prints around in her hand, 'but…'

The picture she handed to me was taken in her back garden. I was sitting out on the lawn in Helen's blue kimono. My eyes were cast downward as I stroked Janus the cat in a rare moment where she would actually sit still.

Laura smiled.

'Taming the wild beast.'

'It doesn't look like me,' I said.

'Only to you, it doesn't.'

I started into a miserable outburst of self-deprecation, trying to convince Laura that even if this particular photo of me was flattering, it was a trick of the light, the angle, that was not the Alberta people saw every day. I was developing a double chin. Mother Ann had told me to stop eating so quickly and so much because she didn't want me to 'end up like her'. I desperately wanted Laura to come back with some soothing compliments. This gesture didn't feel like enough, I wanted her to explain what, if my self-perception was so obscured, did I actually look like to others?

'Did you notice?' she asked, 'none of them, not even Uncle Mel, said my photos were any good.'

23 / DISTANCE YOURSELF FROM
   THE DOG

The day Laura gave up photography, Melvin moved to Berlin. He had decided this on a supposed whim, but Laura suspected he didn't feel important anymore, now that the local theatre company had disbanded due to infighting. Jonathan hosted a going away 'party'. Melvin's relationship with Jade had continued to wither to the point where they remained reluctant friends for the sake of their child. Now almost two, Nina stumbled about the Clemence living room, attempting to climb up her father's leg as he gently pushed her away in favour of a top up to his glass of fizzy wine, some of which Laura slipped into our glasses of lemonade. Valerie passed around a plate of cocktail onions and cheese cubes impaled on toothpicks and looked visibly hurt when Laura said she didn't want any of her 'cock cheese'. Laura wandered about trying to take some candid photographs of her family but when Jonathan snapped at her to get that thing out of his face, I never saw that camera in her hands again.

'She doesn't seem right, that kid,' Laura whispered to me as Nina jumped up and down on the spot humming to herself.

'Seems normal to me,' I said.

Laura pouted and shook her head.

'She knows something I don't.'

I took a large swig of my wine shandy.

'Of course she does, you know things that I don't know, I know things that you don't know, it's normal.'

Laura drummed her fingers, covered in chipped maroon nail polish, on the side of her glass for so long it began to unnerve me.

'I dunno, maybe I just hate kids. I don't like Jade either. Thinks her shit doesn't stink.'

I looked over at Jade, who took a single hors d'oeuvre from Valerie, feigning delight. She carefully removed both the cheese and cocktail onion from the toothpick and dropped them all onto her plate one by one. She stared, revolted, down at her deconstructed creation.

'Maybe I should learn how to cook,' said Laura, who had clearly been preoccupied with what vocation she could take up now that photography was no longer an option.

'But you hate cooking,' I said. 'Remember a few weeks ago when we were trying to make a cake and you couldn't attach the beater to the electric mixer and you got so upset you threw the batter out?'

'Yeah, well, I don't know. Aren't we supposed to be thinking about what we want to do with our lives?'

'I'm trying not to think about anything at the moment,' I said.

Laura said that I was right, that we just needed a distraction.

'Valerie is worried I don't get enough Vitamin D. She says Jonathan is always lying out in the sun because he thinks it keeps him sane. Doesn't seem to be working. But maybe we should get out more.'

Laura convinced me to go back to the creek behind the Durstons. She said we could reclaim the area as our own, that she doubted we would run into Hayley because he was now working full time and had more 'adult' things to do. I knew she wanted to go back there as an excuse to visit Helen, because surely that muddy old creek no longer held any allure for us. I agreed to go, and even drop in on Helen, as long as we made sure Hayley was at work and the garage was open — meaning Bill wasn't home either. Laura observed that I had become an expert in avoidance, that I always considered every possible scenario that would cause me any anxiety. It's exhausting to be this way. I spend so much time strategising over how not to get hurt that I end up hurting myself more. At least when I was at school, when I had Laura to help me, I could maintain a certain amount of functionality.

The exposure therapy worked. I no longer saw the creek as a place of misery and violence. It became a weekend ritual. We stuffed our school bags full of Helen's old clothing and made our way through the bushland, running along in white lace petticoats and peasant blouses, imagining we were the kind of wild ingenues that function just enough and are crazy in palatable amounts, but really we were screaming, obnoxious, dirty, one second crying the next laughing, and when the sounds we made began to merge into this disorienting symphony, neither of us paid attention to who was doing the crying and who was doing the laughing and it didn't even cross my mind that you could do both at once.

We would sit in the shallow water when the summer heat was particularly fierce. Laura was becoming irritated by my habit of sitting in the water fully clothed, particularly on the day I complained that my white cheesecloth dress was becoming transparent. I had to keep pulling the fabric away because the water was making it stick to my body, but once the fabric was loose again it swelled and expanded, making me look like a giant inflatable Michelin woman. The water was simultaneously exposing my fatness and amplifying it. The dress was an external lung that respired inside in a pool of brown muck.

'You've got your togs on underneath yeah? It's just me, just take those stupid clothes off,' said Laura, who was sitting on a broad flat rock on the bank, swinging her legs back and forth in the water. She was wearing a plain black two-piece, her House of Helen couture — a blue velvet slip dress — discarded under a nearby tree. 'See this?' Grabbing folds of skin around the middle and hunching over in an exaggerated manner. 'Who gives a shit?'

'That's skin.'

'No one's coming, you'll be more comfortable.'

'Why aren't you getting in the water?'

'The Red Baron is here,' That was her code word for her period. Named for both Snoopy's nemesis and Laura's grandmaman's (supposed) ex-lover, Manfred von Richthofen.

'So?'

'Haven't you noticed that when you go swimming with a tampon in, it gets waterlogged really quickly? That and I forgot to bring any spares with me. So what am I going to do, free-bleed on Monterey land?' She looked at me with a kind of caution, as though she was uncertain how I would respond to her bringing them up.

'Quiet! They might hear you,' I said, half joking.

'Bullshit, they can't walk that far, not now that poor old Ed has the gout or whatever.'

Laura had been pulling apart a gum leaf and she tossed the tiny pieces into the water where they lay gently on the surface. She looked disappointed at the delicacy of it all.

I asked her what gout was and she began describing a disease akin to leprosy where your limbs go black and fall off and, in retrospect, I believe she was trying to describe gangrene. Apparently, Laura had seen Ed Monterey in the waiting room at the doctor's surgery with crutches and a bandaged foot.

'And Mrs Monterey, she was telling him he had to put the pressure on Frank about the money and that Ed needed to stop scratching the outside of his bandage or he'd make it worse and then he was all: "Stop nagging me, Margaret" like she was the worst thing to ever happen to him.'

'I didn't know her name was Margaret.'

'She's got such a Margaret face, don't you think? So tight and bitchy. She looks like she would carry one of those riding crops around all the time, just to hit people with. I bet she belts Ed around; I bet Ed enjoys it.'

I could tell by the way she was talking that she was making things up again. Since she had confessed in front of Helen that she sometimes lied for attention, Laura had been particularly sensitive to any implication that she might be embellishing. A lot of the time, she just couldn't help it. In these instances, I either had to play along or change the subject. I selected the former in this case because I was curious as to how much she actually knew about the Montereys. She had gone to visit Helen without me knowing on at least one occasion. Even on the days we passed the Durstons on the way to the creek, and it looked as though Helen would be home alone, Laura would never suggest we check in on her. On one occasion she grabbed me by the wrist and pulled me in the direction of the creek, telling me not to look back until we reached the other side.

'Did you notice there weren't any horses around on the way here?'

I asked, hoping she would tell me if she'd given any more thought to our theory that Helen and Ed were siblings.

'That's basically my entire point, Al. This Frank guy they were talking about at the doctors, he owes them money, probably for a horse. They're getting old, probably retiring, probably buying a beach house or something boring like that.'

'Did you ask her?' I immediately regretted asking the question, and was already thinking of ways I could mould it into something else, like 'did you ask Margaret about her horses?' or 'did you ask Val if you could go out this afternoon?' neither of which seemed like a natural query. Laura knew I meant Helen.

'No. I didn't want to upset her.'

I nodded.

'That's true. It's a stupid idea anyway — '

' — I asked Hayley, though.'

I wrapped my arms around my middle the way I did when I needed fortification, in the way that made me look to most people like I had a stomach ache. I hadn't wanted to ask her if these secret visits were true. I wanted her to hate Hayley. She even gave me the impression she did when she revealed to our friends at Rachael's party that she felt remorse for not defending me when he hit me. But I couldn't stop thinking about the photographs of Helen, the fact that he was there when Laura said he'd left, the fact that I tried to elude: that he wasn't wearing a shirt.

I swallowed three times before I was able to say anything.

'When did you ask him?'

'A few weeks ago — Saturday before last — when you went to your dad's.' She stared at me. Inspected my face. 'It was bad, so don't get upset about it. You're lucky you weren't there, because he got really mad with me.'

Was she saying that Hayley getting angry at her was worse than what he did to me? I stared at my thick thighs jutting from the water, convincing myself that this was in fact an enormous free-flowing river that I had dammed up with my bulk, that I had polluted it with my decaying extraneous flab. All I could do was apologise to her, for reasons I couldn't quite articulate, I said sorry, sorry, I'm sorry. I told her I was sorry and that she could, of course, do whatever she liked, that I knew I was always flaking out on her, that if she'd asked me I would have probably not wanted to go anyway, that she didn't need my permission.

She thanked me for saying so. Then:

'Helen wants me to pretend to be her daughter.'

I asked her why. She said people pretend to be something to somebody all the time. I asked her if she was okay with that.

'Well, yeah,' she said, 'I don't have a mother.'

Again I told her I was sorry, that it was stupid of me to have not realised that. I had assumed that because she had me, she didn't need someone else. But even as I said this, I resented Helen, I knew it was Laura's company she needed, not mine. I resented Hayley, I resented the times Mother Ann would insist we drop in on Pa at the shop and I would see Hayley out of the corner of my eye and smell petrol and wet grass and feel something like desire.

Laura carefully waded into the creek and sat down next to me, laying her head on my shoulder. I looked at both our legs side by side. Our knees sticking out of the water. Mine were twice the size of hers. I recalled the time I overheard Mother Ann tell Aunt Julia that I had 'thick legs'. Laura closed her eyes. I needed to look outside of my insecurities. The weight of her head on my shoulder made the tension in my muscles relax. Of course she needed a parental figure, one that would both look her in the eye and take an interest in her general wellbeing. Even if Helen never moved from that couch, never stepped out of her house ever again, Laura would come and let her play with her hair and talk about ghosts. Laura would consult her like an oracle. I remember the picture on the Durston's fridge of Helen holding baby Hayley in her arms. I could imagine her as the blind woman from our nameless film, her face framed by dark soft nineteen seventies curls, the dramatic black and blue eye makeup, the strange intermingling of vulnerability and power.

'She still makes me nervous, Helen does,' Laura said in a soft voice.

I placed my arm around her shoulder. I told her that when I first met Helen, she had frightened me.

'She could barely hold her head up. She seemed happy to meet me but the next second she wanted me and Hayley to go away.'

'Then the horse thing happened?'

I nodded.

'When I took the blanket to her she was so nice. She seemed awake and interested in me, interested in what was going on around her. But when I went when you were at your dad's, I didn't ask. I just showed up. I needed to. Helen was asleep. I told Hayley I just needed someone to talk to because you weren't around. It's like, when you go away, I kind of shut down. I don't like myself. So, when you're not here, I need them. But I couldn't, you know, describe it all to Hayley like that. I asked him if Helen was asleep, could I just talk to him for a bit and he said okay and we went into his room and I asked him if it was true that Helen was related to Ed Monterey. He said he had no idea what I was talking about and why would I care anyway? I asked him if he'd ever seen the ghost of his Great Aunt Vera and he said no, that his mother was sick in the head and she made all that up. It's true that his family and the Montereys hate each other, but that's just because the petrol fumes were giving Margaret a headache so one day Ed marched over there and had a go at Bill and Bill said something like: "well it's definitely not what's killing your horses, mate." So then I asked Hayley if he was sure that was it, that it was that simple. He said he didn't know what I wanted him to say, that I needed to stop thinking everything is to do with me when it wasn't, that it was none of my business, that he only puts up with it because Helen said she saw me as a daughter. When I asked him what was wrong with that he said I was being selfish because she can barely be a mother to him and we were both batshit. And it's true.'

'I know what you mean,' I said. Followed by more apologies. 'I know I'm not the only one with — the whatcha-callits — neuroses.'

'But you want to be,' she said, standing up.

I did. I did want to be the only one. I had convinced myself that if I was certifiably crazy, that it would be the one thing that set me apart. Even if pain alone made me unique. I looked at Laura and nodded, to let her know I understood. Laura nodded back, as though relieved I wasn't hurt. She almost looked proud.

'Then what did Hayley do?'

'He grabbed me by the shoulders, but really gentle and kind of, steered towards the door. And didn't say goodbye or anything. As usual.' Laura dried herself off and put her dress back on, a slight smile on her face.

I didn't want to hear any more.

'Going?' I asked.

Laura was already walking away.

'Yep,' she said, pulling her towel over her head like the Virgin Mary.

As we caught sight of the Durston's back yard, we saw Helen standing by the fence.

'Shit, what's she doing outside?' Laura began to walk faster like a nurse power walking down a hospital corridor to restrain a wayward patient.

I stumbled after her.

'Maybe the sun would do her good? I asked, becoming increasingly out of breath, 'Vitamin D?'

Helen was plucking the branches off a wild privet shrub. She saw us and waved us over. I scanned the backyard for signs of Bill.

'She wouldn't be waving to us if Bill was around,' Laura whispered, intercepting my avoidance strategy.

I brushed some grass off Laura's backside. She did the same for me.

'Is everything okay?' I asked Helen. She had one hand clutched around the barbed wire fence. She looked from me to Laura, from Laura to me. She was wearing a purple cheesecloth dress and her hair was wet, dripping around her shoulders. She had aged a lot in the last few years. She had lines around her eyes and her neck looked wiry and fragile. She was even thinner than before. Or maybe I was only used to seeing her indoors, in the dark. Her eyes looked red, the skin underneath them was dry and flaking. She kept one hand on the barbed wire and the other reached out for Laura, who held it tight. It was like they had become frozen in time. The sky had become slightly overcast, and there was a ringing in my ear. I could hear every sound around me, a lawn mower, a truck pulling into Durston's Garage, the discordant caw and melodic whistle of a butcher bird, a door slamming. I was standing outside of things again, like in the rain that day with Hayley. I thought maybe this was the antithesis of what I felt when I saw that alien light shine through Laura's window as she lay as if dead on her bedroom floor. Maybe, now, she was watching me, collapsed on the ground, while she experienced the most defining moment of her life.

'Well yes, I suppose so. But you don't love him anyway,' I heard Helen say before I returned my attention to Laura who was on the ground, her legs sprawled out underneath her like a ragdoll that had been tossed aside by a boisterous child. Helen was inspecting her hand, the one that was gripping the barbed wire fence. There was a wound in her palm from which a small bead of blood was forming.

'I was just telling Laura — I buried Agnes this morning.'

I thought for a moment.

'But isn't your mother —'

'—the dog. The dog died, Al,' Laura snapped, wrapping her towel around her head again, like armour.

Helen invited us in and slowly made us some tea, while Laura and I sat on the couch, silent. Laura in her virginal shroud with grass and dirt all over her legs, me in that stupid white dress, a towel around my waist, both so waterlogged a large wet spot was already spreading over the brown fabric. I stood up when Helen returned and gestured apologetically towards the stain.

'Oh don't worry about that, sit down, sit down,' she said, squeezing in next to Laura. 'This ugly old thing has seen much worse.'

I apologised again anyway for good measure, then asked: 'Where did you bury her? Agnes?'

'Out by the agapanthus. She loved the agapanthus. Used to bat at the fronds with her paw. She was a very old girl. Must have died in her sleep. Hayley doesn't know yet. He and Bill left for work early and she must have just slipped away before I woke up. I was digging the hole when Bill came home for lunch. He never liked the dog but Hayley — he's not going to take it very well. I was covered in dirt and she was a fat little thing, hard to lift, so I'm a bit sore now but what else could I do?'

'You did what you had to do,' said Laura, still slightly preoccupied.

'I should have waited,' said Helen, nibbling at her thumb nail, 'but I didn't want him to see her like that.'

'No,' I said, wiping tears away from my face with the edge of my towel, 'It would be too hard to just leave her there, waiting for him. I

— I really liked Agnes. When I was little, I saw her a fair bit but…I always wanted my own dog, but when I see how hard it is when they…I don't think I could.'

'You don't want to feel worse than you already do? I'll get some tissues.' Helen wandered off towards her bedroom.

Laura was still staring into space. The only sound in the room was my awful sniffling.

Helen returned with a box of tissues and I worked my way through a great many, until I held in my hand a wad of mucus and tears. I managed a soft laugh.

'I'm just leaking everywhere aren't I? I'm sorry.'

'Don't say you're sorry,' said Laura in her stern yet nurturing tone. It was a relief to hear. I thought she was angry with me. But still, her eyes were dry as she took a sip of her tea. She had yet to look either of us in the eye.

'Does it hurt all the time?' Helen asked, sitting in front of us on the floor, cross-legged.

Laura was still not responding, so I nodded.

'What does it feel like?' Helen asked.

'Like I'm not supposed to be this way,' I said. 'Like something has always been wrong and I don't know what it is.'

'It feels like death,' Laura said. 'It's like I force myself to come alive and then I'm dead over and over. It's like someone kills me and then brings me back to life and reminds me to keep smiling and be nice all the time or else.'

'It's like everything, every small thing that happens is a tragedy,' I added. 'Like I'm grieving every moment. Like something that I love dies every instant but I'm not even allowed to remember what it was or why the face of every stranger scares me, that being alone scares me, that being in a crowd scares me, being alive scares me.'

'It's like I've got a million pieces of rope tied all around me and they're all so tight but I have to try and keep moving, and pretend, and I'm just — really tired,' said Laura, pulling her towel off her head and throwing it to the ground.

Helen nodded. 'I know. But it might be better this way. It didn't happen to me until I was, I don't know, thirty? Hayley was only small. He hasn't known me any other way. But if you're both feeling this when you're both so young, that gives you time. If you've got the time, both of you…'

Hayley pushed his way into the room, still in his work apron, two heavy looking bags of groceries draped over each forearm. He looked at us in our big wet huddle and removed himself to the kitchen where he started loudly putting things away.

Laura stood up. 'We shouldn't be here when you tell him,' she said.

To leave as we usually did, out the back door, we had to walk through the kitchen. Hayley glared at Laura.

'What did you do? I told you —'

'Your dog's dead,' she said, quietly, before grabbing my hand and pulling me outside.

We walked in silence. When we reached Laura's front door, she opened it and gestured for me to walk through.

'Are you sure?'

She nodded. 'I'm always sure.'

24 / CARNELIAN AND ONYX

In the Last Year With Laura, I dyed my hair red. Mother Ann was, for some reason, very serious about me not colouring my hair until I was sixteen. We sat on Laura's bathroom floor, covered in old towels. My head ached from the smell of ammonia, and when I rinsed the dye out in the shower it was like blood was running down every inch of my body. I finally felt what it was like to be a girl in a horror movie, Carrie at the prom, Sally laughing with joy at the end of *The Texas Chainsaw Massacre*. I ran my fingers through my hair then reached my arm out and let the blood run down my arm, like I'd just smashed it through a window. I was the final girl.

When I got out of the shower and described it to Laura, she held up her palms. They were stained red.

'Those plastic gloves did jack shit,' she said. 'My turn.'

When she exited the shower, she told me all about her black blood.

We let our hair dry out in the sun. We lay on the grass, fanning our hair out, entwining it, black and red, red and black. Finally, a clear contrast. Valerie shuffled out of her flat, head down, in her slippers and dressing gown. She shouted at us to make sure we didn't 'get a bloody melanoma' before entering the main house. I pointed out that it wasn't like Valerie to still be in her pyjamas in the middle of the day. Laura said she was unpredictable.

'It's like she thinks because she can't see me, I can't see her. I remember when I was really little, playing hide and seek in pre-school, and I would never actually go and hide anywhere, I would just put my hands over my eyes and say: "I've got my eyes closed, you can't see me!" No one ever bothered to tell Val it doesn't work that way.' Laura pulled a lighter and a soft pack of Peter Stuyvesants from her pocket. She had begun stealing from Jonathan's stash. He was known to buy cartons in bulk. She lit two cigarettes in her mouth and handed one to me. I gestured towards Valerie's doorstep:

'That ceramic tortoise is new.'

Laura snorted. 'She had a big fight with Jonathan about it. He said he didn't care that it was technically outside her door, that it was still his property and he got to decide how it was decorated and he hated the tortoise because he felt like it was watching him whenever he went out in the garden. Then things got quiet for a while but I'm sure at some point Val asked Jonathan if she disgusted him and he said something like: "yes, I can't help it." It's like Jonathan spends his whole life in a room with a locked door and Val just keeps on throwing herself against it.'

Laura had finally got a new bed, at least, Jonathan's old one. She was pleased in the end because it was king sized and she had been asking for a meagre double for the last four years. We had spread ourselves across Laura's (now enormous) duvet with a large packet of potato chips and a bottle of wine, which she said had been sitting in the back of the fridge for months so no one would miss it. I took a sip. It was a tart chardonnay, old and revolting but it would do. We finished the bottle off quickly, in relative silence, as we watched an episode of *Neon Genesis Evangelion*. Before the show was over, Laura grabbed the remote control from my lap and switched the TV off.

'When you weren't at school last Wednesday, I called Ann to find out where you were and she said you were asleep because going to the psychologist took a lot out of you. "Like you could imagine, Laura," she said. Like she assumed I knew.'

My first impulse was to tell her she was the last person who should be demanding honesty from me. It had been almost eight months since Agnes died, since Laura pushed past Hayley out that door with such resolve. I thought she had finally chosen me. When, that night, she asked me to stay with her, sleep beside her, we decided never again, that whenever we left the Durstons we left distraught, confused, exhausted. Never again. I was so relieved that I even forgave her for the things she continued to conceal from me, that I was willing to ignore now that my hair was red and hers was black.

I was drunk, and I could have very easily said all of this immediately, loudly, with tears, right in her face. Instead I asked her to give me a cigarette and we stumbled over to her window and Laura swore as the latch holding the bay window closed was stuck and as she finally pushed the window open a warm breeze rushed in and I could see the roof of my house that from up there made me wish it would never be my house again. We sat on the ledge blowing smoke into the night. I heard Louis screaming.

'Will I die before I get to see the inside of your house?' Laura asked.

I said I didn't know.

'You can hear that, right? Why would you want to?'

'Why would I want to? I'm not sure, Al, maybe because you are my best friend and we've known each other for seven years and you've never let me step even a fucking millimetre inside that gate and you're seeing a psychologist now?'

'I didn't tell you because I didn't want you to worry about that stuff. I know you get sick of me crying and talking shit about myself.'

'It's that — that *talk* —I get sick of,' Laura said, flicking the ash out of her cigarette, the light breeze blowing some of it back inside.

I said that if she really wanted to know, I had an appointment with a woman named Sally-Anne Lindquist. Mother Ann came into the room with me at first, to help me feel more at ease. Sally-Anne seemed aloof and tired. She told Mother Ann she had a teenage daughter too, she understood. They talked about me like I wasn't there. I knew who her daughter was, she was Sarah Lindquist, the School Captain. There was talk she would probably end up dux of the school by the end of the year. She was a debating champion. She was going to be a doctor. Once Mother Ann had left us alone, Sally-Anne said to me:

'I believe you are anxious. Moodiness is a natural response to the growth hormone. I also think you might be exaggerating matters a bit — my daughter does the same — but if we do some relaxation exercises you might be able to manage things a bit better and give your mum a break, huh?' She laid me down on a massage table and put on a CD of whale sounds and told me to imagine a golden ball of light spreading throughout my body, and to clear my mind of all thoughts. I said I couldn't possibly clear my mind of all thoughts and think about a golden ball of light at the same time and she sounded irritated and said she meant focus on just the ball of light and not let my mind wander to things that were troubling me and at that point one of the whales on the CD let out a mournful yelp and I immediately thought it had lost its baby. Then I thought about everyone in my life and how they must hate me.

Laura took all this in for a moment and then burst out laughing.

'She's fucking useless, isn't she?' She had been taken to see Sally-Anne Lindquist too. 'It was a while back, after Uncle Mel's going away party. Jonathan told me to stop taking photos and I let it stew and stew until I felt sick and so the next day I just asked, I asked him why he doesn't give a shit, I asked him how many million dollars he's paying Val to be his house bitch, how he couldn't run this house by just floating around all the time not saying anything, just, existing. So a few days later, Val tells me that Jonathan would like me to seek some professional assistance for my unruliness and there you go — Sally-Anne Lindquist — whale sounds, crystals, Swedish furniture. She told me exactly the same thing she told you.'

'I'm sorry, Laura,' I said.

'You'll regret saying that in a minute.'

She made me sit on the edge of her bed. She placed a box of tissues next to me. She took my empty mug and ran across the hall to the bathroom, rinsed the wine out of it and filled it with water. She placed it on her bedside table.

'Helen is in hospital again. Hayley told me not to tell anyone. And I didn't want you to worry. Bill's gone away again. And I didn't want to go, but he sounded so sad.'

'Hayley's an arsehole,' I mumbled into the mug of water. It still tasted like chardonnay.

'Yup,' said Laura. 'Guess I'm just like Val.'

I breathed in and out in that broken, shuddering way.

Laura put her arm around me.

'It's okay Al, it's okay. We can stop talking about it if you want.'

I said no. That I was tired of not talking about it. 'If you're not going to be my friend anymore just get it out of the way now.'

'This isn't about you. That's a good thing,' she said as she pulled her t-shirt over her head. Her chest was covered in marks, the kind of bruise that I made with my own mouth when I was too small to understand, and Mother Ann said to never do such an awful thing again.

I lightly touched one of the marks near her collar bone.

'Did it hurt?'

She shook her head.

'You know things like that don't hurt me.'

'Did you like it?'

'Sort of.'

'Are you going to do it again?' I asked.

Laura shook her head again. I held out her shirt for her and slipped it back over her head. She walked, almost stumbled, over to her wardrobe. From under a pile of clothes that she's tossed inside she produced the Monterey's horseshoe cross. 'We need to bury this.'

I was sitting with Louis in front of the television. He let me sit on the couch now. Before he wouldn't let me near the thing, even though he never sat there himself, preferring to pace back and forth in front of the screen, flapping his hands, the controls on the front of the VCR close at hand so he could rewind the same small section over and over. He'd broken the remote control long ago. Mother Ann had begun trusting me to 'babysit', which sounded odd considering I was a sixteen-year-old minding a fourteen-year-old.

One of the things I resented most throughout our childhood was that Louis began to covet all my belongings if he took a shine to them. And once something becomes Louis', you never get to so much as touch that object again. So, when he chose my old VHS of *Return to Oz* to watch, I was pleased. Even though I knew he wasn't going to watch the whole thing.

I first saw *Return to Oz* when I was four. A sequel to *The Wizard of Oz*, the film begins with Aunt Em and Uncle Henry deciding they have had enough of Dorothy going on and on about imaginary nonsense, so she's sent off in a rickety old horse and buggy to a big, black Edwardian hospital. To forget. There, the kindly, beardy doctor waxes lyrical about the wonders of the modern age. Electricity. He all but rolls his eyes at Dorothy's stories of tin men and talking lions, but then has the gall to introduce her to the electro-shock machine by trying to convince her it had a face. 'See the dials there?' he asks. 'Those are his eyes.' He decided to speak to her in her own language before he deprived her of it for good.

Louis froze.

'Who's at the door? It's Daddy. Daddy's back from his holiday.'

I shushed him.

'You've got to be?'

'…quiet.'

He liked to finish my sentences. I petted him on the shoulder.

'Like a big senior boy.'

He nodded.

'Not like a baby.'

It was Laura. Her voice sounded strange.

'Sorry, Al, I saw your mum leave a while ago and I can't tell you this stuff on the phone, please?'

Louis was still carrying on so I slipped outside to join her. She looked like she had been crying for some time. She grabbed hold of me and buried her face in my shoulder.

'It's so fucked up. Even the way I found out is fucked up.'

I took her inside to my bedroom without a word, without even caring about what she thought of my awful house, my screaming brother. She was in a stupor and didn't even notice Louis who was asking her repeatedly who she was until I locked the door on him. I felt a brief surge of responsibility. My turn to carry her.

Laura curled up on my bed and buried her head in her hands. This wasn't the breakdown at the Agricultural Fair, this was a Laura devastated beyond my understanding. She didn't seem able to talk so I put her head in my lap and let her go. Louis returned frequently to bang on the door and ask me who was in there with me, and I kept on shouting at him to go away. I thought about the marks on Laura's chest, whether it had something to do with that. I wondered if Hayley had hurt her again. We had buried the horseshoe cross by the creek. Laura believed that by doing so, everything would be better. Eventually, she sat up, pulled her jumper over her hand and wiped her nose.

'Jessie called me. She heard from her mum who heard it from someone…I have no idea. It's got to be because I took the cross.'

I shook my head.

'The cross means nothing, Laura.'

Laura was furious.

'I took the cross and now Helen's dead. How can you say it's not important? I took it out from under the couch and it's all my fault. It was keeping her alive.'

Louis was beating his fists on the door.

'Louis not now, fuck off!' I screamed, throwing the door open and pushing him so hard his feet gave way underneath him and as I turned to slam the door in his face again he slapped me hard across the back. Laura ran forward to try and pull me away. I got up and shoved Louis, this time so hard he hit his head on the door frame. He ran out into the living room, screaming and throwing himself on the couch, banging his head against the wicker armrest that creaked and crackled with every blow.

'Shut up shut up shut up!' I was throwing anything I could find at him and Laura was yelling at me to stop and was pulling my hands away from my head to stop me hitting myself and she was trying so hard to restrain my arms that I thought she would have leapt onto my back if I hadn't then collapsed with her to the floor, where we screamed and screamed until we were exhausted and numb.

Mother Ann already knew what had happened by the time she got home. She gave each of us one of her special 'coping pills', that made us so tired we slept crushed together in my single bed right through the night. In the morning, she made us a large breakfast but neither of us could eat.

'You both must feel so groggy,' she said. 'A tiny quarter of a benzo when everything is too much and I sleep like a baby.'

'Does Father Robert take them?' I asked.

'Of course. I need very little, but he takes a large dose when he's having an episode – and other things as well. I mean, I assume he still takes them, I wouldn't know, now.'

'Then why don't I have my own medication?'

'Darling something awful has just happened. We'll talk about that another day. This is the kind of sadness that will pass. You're both sad for Hayley I know but you didn't know Helen all that well, did you? She wasn't a well lady from what I've heard.'

Louis walked up to the table, cautious. When he was sure I wasn't going to shout or push or slap him, he took a seat next to Laura. She looked up at him and smiled.

I spent the next night at Laura's. We decided that even though Mother Ann meant well, it was too difficult to pretend we didn't really know Helen. Laura said that now she had been inside my house, she could understand the difficulty of both living in a home without privacy and living in one with too much. We chose the latter as we reasoned we could continue to self-medicate with cigarettes and alcohol and violent films. Laura's room became a bunker. We would sleep during the day and watch television late into the night, which is when we saw *Possession*. Laura and I sat swigging from a bottle of rum from the back of Jonathan's liquor cabinet and watched Sam Neil and Isabelle Adjani scream at each other, neglect their child, and cause a scene at a cafe. 'Jesus! Jesus! Jesus! Jesus!' Isabelle shouted. Every time she screamed and sweated and cried and trembled she was very tired after. Then it would start again. Sam hit her to try and snap her out of it and she wandered down the street with blood pouring from her mouth. She cut her neck with an electric knife and he did the same just to prove he could.

Then, around the middle of the film, Isabelle had an episode in a subway tunnel. She screeched and retched, vomiting a milk-like substance all over her blue dress. Then the same stuff started pouring out from between her legs — a kind of alien miscarriage. A painful catharsis. Laura had to pause the film at that point. She said she had forgotten how to breathe. Once the film was over, we rewound that scene again and again. I wondered, how can a Berlin subway be that quiet in the middle of the day? Why, also, had no one come along, carried Isabelle off to hospital or at least looked at her in a disparaging way? Now I realise. The film was allowing her to have this crucial, intimate moment without any critical bystanders there to tell her she is foul, inhuman, monstrous. This is why I scream into my pillow, why I punch the tiles when I'm in the shower and, if anyone hears, make the excuse that I dropped something, a bottle of shampoo. The two sounds are nearly indistinguishable —heavy and hollow.

When Laura and I ran to the bathroom to throw up all that rum, we had to run the shower to cover up the sounds of us retching, me into the toilet, Laura on all fours under the shower. When we were done, I joined her under the cold water.

'That's the last one,' Laura mumbled, struggling to keep her head up.

26 / SOMEONE'S MOTHER

Helen was to have a private funeral. Family only. I was relieved. I knew Laura would be disappointed. I tried to call her but I kept getting a message telling me the number I had dialled was disconnected. I went and knocked on her door. No one answered. All the windows were closed. I looked up into Laura's bedroom and saw only the dark, the kind of dark I would see as I sat as a child watching that house, wishing it were mine. I looked up at the window again. The house looked smaller than it did back then, but just as empty.

I hardly remember my last year of high school. Mother Ann would pull up to the gate in the morning and have to sit there, the car idling away, until I stopped snivelling and protesting that I couldn't possibly go in there, but eventually I did. Most days. Mother Ann gave me lots of long-winded lectures about how when we fall on hard times, when we think we can't go on and all those other tired diatribes about resilience, that I should think about the woman whose baby was stuck under a car. She was able to lift the car clean off that baby because we humans aren't made to just give up.

I've heard that story so many times over the years that I'm sure it must be an urban legend. I'm more inclined to believe that story about the couple who are driving alone on a deserted street at night when they hear on the radio someone had escaped from the looney bin. The report warned everyone to be on the lookout for a man that had a hook for a hand. When the couple get home, they get out of their car to find a hook dangling from the door handle. In some versions it's stuck to the roof. Sometimes the couple survive, sometimes they don't.

I was beginning to feel that my inclination to 'just push through' was not to save myself, but to destroy myself completely. I wondered if maybe I would die of an aneurysm in my sleep, like Philomena Rankin. Maybe when it was finally all too much I would just burst into flames and start haunting Laura's old bedroom.

When a new family finally moved into the house across the road, I had the temptation to ask them if they knew where the previous owners went. Did they know them? But I couldn't because I couldn't walk up to a stranger and start a conversation. Laura used to do that for me, Laura used to get that kind of information. I had been left with no one who would understand that in order to speak to them over the phone I needed to let their phone ring twice and have them call me back. I couldn't hide with my fingers in my ears and have someone make whatever, or whoever was troubling me go away.

Jessie and Rachael looked out for me at school, sat with me at lunchtime, made small talk. They told me how shitty Hayley was looking when they saw him around, or at the fruit shop. Jessie said he looked stoned all the time, that she wondered why Pa didn't fire him because she'd heard a guy in our grade called Brendon Harris stole a whole bag of kiwifruit the other day and Hayley totally saw and totally didn't care.

Jessie asked me whether Hayley knew anything about where Laura went. I said I doubted it.

'She liked him though, didn't she? Did you even ask him?'

'What made you think she liked him?' I asked.

'At Rachael's sleepover a few years ago when we were drunk and Laura and I said sorry to each other for the dumb shit I pulled in primary school, she told me — she said that she wanted to hate him because of what he did to you, but she couldn't because she loved him.

Actually, she said she loved both of you the same. But she said that if I told you that you would probably hate her.'

Rachael suggested to Jessie that maybe I didn't want to talk about this stuff anymore. Jessie apologised but she added that if she were me, she wouldn't shut up about it.

'I hold massive grudges,' she said, 'and it helps, but only if I talk about them. If I keep it all inside I would just be in a huge fucking rage all the time.'

She kept on like this for a while, talking about how honesty changed her life and that I needed to trust her and Rachael to help me through all this so I could finish year twelve because she knew I could do it, that I was smart if I just tried harder, that maybe thinking about what I wanted to do after school would be the key to me moving on with my life, that I couldn't just stay in this shithole forever. All this fake sincerity bored me. I wasn't going to tell them what I was feeling. I couldn't articulate it even if I tried. I couldn't expel my anguish onto two girls I only hung around with out of necessity.

'Hayley shaved his head, he looks absolutely mental,' Jessie added as a rushed footnote to her long-winded rant.

Pa decided to retire. He was training Hayley to be the on-site manager. Pa told me Hayley had been 'asking after me' with a nudge and wink that he couldn't stop himself from doing. I had been avoiding him as much as I could over the years which meant the smallest of small talk, dodging kisses on the cheek on special occasions, wearing as many clothes as possible in his presence and sweating even more than usual at family gatherings. Ma took me aside one day and said that for Mother Ann's sake, I should try really hard with my exams.

'She'll need you to help her one day, you know,' she said, like I had already overstayed my welcome. That when a girl turns eighteen she must be cast out into the world and only return when she can be of use.

I held out long enough to get my high school certificate. Then, when that car-lifting survival mechanism started slowing down, my body went with it. I went to bed, only to wake up occasionally, when Mother Ann took me to the doctor who told me that I might be happier if I lost a little weight and just walked through life with my head held high, insinuating that I was to pretend everything was okay and if I did that long enough, maybe it would be.

I was referred to a psychiatrist named Brenda Nab. She was a middle-aged woman, who wore glasses with multi-coloured frames that looked like they came from a brand called something like Funky Specs. When I sat down opposite her and told her how I felt, she cooed and said uh-huh and yeah and nodded the way people do when they're not listening.

'People haven't been very nice to you, have they?'

I had walked into Brenda Nab's office determined not to cry, but I did. She cooed again like a mother pigeon from a children's book and passed me a box of tissues covered in puppies. I said I wasn't sleeping well, that I couldn't bear the sound of the toads rattling outside the window, that whenever I did manage to fall asleep, I had nightmares. I told her about one of my them:

'I was lying in my bed in the dark and I heard a deep cough — like a man's cough. My door creaked open and I could just make out his outline. He was tall. I ran at him and smashed his face in with the bottom of a heavy, brass lamp. I didn't see what I was doing to his face, but I could tell it was caving in. It felt easy to kill someone in the dark – to keep on hitting and hitting. Then I was suddenly in my old house, the house we lived in when I was small. We moved out when I was seven. I can't remember much about the place but in my dream I recognised the hallway and the orange laminate in the kitchen. There was the taste of nicotine in my mouth. Then everything went dark again. I started to wander about aimlessly, then I heard a voice, I think it was a little boy. It was as though I had walked in on him mid-sentence. He said he had just turned four. He had two dogs called Toby and Badger. His dad was working in London. He said we could have cake once Daddy was home. Then he said: "Mummy is very clever. She makes films and art and she tells me stories all the time." Then his voice trailed off and I was crawling on my hands and knees, stabbing at the carpet with a blunt pencil. I heard my mother tell me to go back to sleep, that it wasn't my birthday yet. I told her I was having beautiful visions of the future. She told me to stop joking about that when we both knew I had nothing ahead of me. I told her I was not a joke. I said this over and over again. Then I woke up.'

All of the kindness, no matter how superficial, had disappeared from Brenda Nab's face. She said it seemed my subconscious was telling me I wanted to succeed and have a nuclear family and the only way I could do that was to stop exaggerating normal emotions that everyone has. She called it Histrionic Personality Disorder. She gave me a script for some pills that stopped my dreams but made me perpetually exhausted. I would spend most days lying in bed under the covers with my fingers in my ears. When I went back to see Brenda Nab, she said it would be better if she referred me to a colleague that was an expert in my 'sort of problems'. His name was Doctor Brunner. He was a murderer.

27 / PARIS, TEXAS

I slept the year away. I slept through the year I imagined everybody else my age was spending getting fancy degrees or backpacking around Europe and working part-time menial jobs and saving up for a car and fucking a lot.

For my eighteenth birthday, I got my dog. I called her Camille because it's a French name. She smelled like heaven and the pads on her paws were smooth and she loved me. She slept in my bed and I didn't care if I had no party, that Pa had come over with Ma to gift me some money to 'spend on something helpful' and Pa said Hayley said 'happy birthday' and my whole body hurt and that night I lay in bed, Camille lying on my chest, her warm breath puffing rhythmically against my neck. I felt her heartbeat and she felt mine and we both felt (temporarily) safe.

Mother Ann got me some work experience at the primary school library. Jane Forbes, the librarian, was a friend of my mothers. She had a daughter named Freda who shared a taxi with Louis to the training facility they attended. They were learning art and crafts. Louis had developed a love of painting large bright portraits of his favourite fictional characters and Freda made elaborate collages with images cut from magazines – elaborate and intricately constructed Frankenstein's monsters — a Pitbull terrier's head on the limbless torso of a super-model with the muscular hairy legs of an actor caught by the paparazzi kayaking in Fiji.

Going back to my old primary school was strange. Everything seemed so much smaller. I felt like a monster stomping through a movie set. I was Godzilla. I was Gamera. I imagined Jane Forbes would talk to other members of staff about how she didn't know what to do with me, that she didn't really have any jobs to keep me occupied and they would all agree on how pathetic it was that I was essentially going back to primary school after just completing high school, that I couldn't drive yet, that I hadn't gone to university.

It was true that I had very little to do at the library. I re-shelved books then hid in a corner and read a book of my own when the place was full of children. Jane asked if I would like to read to a year one class and I said no. The six-year-olds would laugh at me. They would talk about me behind my back. I kept going to the library twice a week for three months. Often Mother Ann would call in sick for me, because I was sleeping or I had had an episode the night before and was drugged up on benzos and all the while so guilty that I couldn't drive yet, that I couldn't go to university, so the former was remedied. Slowly. Mother Ann taught me how to drive in her old station wagon and I found that being on the road didn't feel as dangerous when you were in control. I took lessons with a patient grandfatherly man (who I thought was much better than Pa and what a grandfather should be) and got my licence on the first try, only because I was tested on the quiet country roads and was never exposed to any particularly challenging situations.

Camille soon became a large, gangling puppy who had more energy than I could help her expel and I felt guilty. I tried training her but I gave her so many treats she just got fat, but she loved me and sometimes in the middle of the night I would wake from a nightmare and find her head on my chest as though to say: 'None of it was real. Listen to my breathing. I am here.' I kissed her on the head and whispered that she was special and that she was going to save my life.

I took up another volunteer position at the town Film Society where I was the youngest person there by about forty years and my suggestions were greeted with disgust so I would sit and sell tickets at the door, never looking up, hoping no one I knew from school would come in and they didn't. No young people wanted to see *My Fair Lady* or *Driving Miss Daisy*. I couldn't imagine myself ever having a paid job. At least in a voluntary position, I could call in sick as many times as I needed and no one would care. I didn't really have anything to lose. At the Film Society, I was paid in DVD rental vouchers from Barry's shop, the only shop I could go into anymore. Once, Barry even smiled at me as I rented five horror films at once. It was a knowing smile, as though he'd known what Laura and I used to do with his tapes.

I never actually watched the films shown at the Film Society. After selling the tickets I would go around the back of the RSL Hall to my car and smoke a few Marlboro Menthol cigarettes and return in time for the intermission where I was to oversee the selling of soft drinks, potato chips, Jaffas and homemade cup-cakes from a kiosk that was only a little wider than my hips while the loud speaker played the theme from *A View to a Kill* by Duran Duran on repeat until the film resumed. I frequently gave people the wrong change. One night, I had left my mobile phone in the car during my smoke break and when I went to go home there were three missed calls and a voice message from Mother Ann saying Pa had had a heart attack and he was dead. I lit a cigarette and laughed and laughed and laughed.

I couldn't even pretend to cry about Pa's death in front of Mother Ann and Ma. The morning of the funeral I was calm but only after taking two benzos. Mother Ann couldn't decide what earrings to wear and I just kept shrugging and Louis had got his hands on a spray-bottle full of water and was spraying us like we were potted plants and cackling. Mother Ann suddenly snapped (at me) and said:

'Alberta, you cry every single bloody day and your grandfather is dead and—' Louis hit her right in the eye with a sharp jet of water. Wiping tears and water from her eyes she turned to me. 'I know you never thought much of your pa but please don't cause a scene.'

'I don't cause scenes,' I said.

'You do when you're drunk. Be careful at the wake.'

'I'm watering the plants!' Louis called from the next room.

'I really am sad, you know. I've taken two benzos — you know they make me dopey and a bit numb. I would cry if I could,' I said. She gave me a brief, stiff hug. She was angry that I couldn't be the person she needed me to be.

My job during the funeral service was to hold Louis' arm at the back of the crowd and keep him quiet. I felt like I was in a film, some mysterious figure from the deceased person's past who didn't want to be seen by the other mourners because, god damn it, hadn't I caused enough trouble already?

I kept my sunglasses on so everyone assumed I was crying. I was to buy Louis' silence with snacks and a new book about the history of animated films, pulled from Mother Ann's stash of emergency presents. Mother Ann bribed Louis with gifts the way I bribed Camille with treats. Every day was Christmas for both of them.

Despite the distractions, not long into the service Louis began to groan and whimper. I tried to quiet him by putting my hand over his mouth. He wriggled out of my grasp and lunged into the crowd. There was some commotion and murmuring before I saw Hayley gently lead Louis away. They sat down together on a concrete bench as Pa was lowered into the ground.

When it was all over, Louis ran to Mother Ann and grabbed her around the waist. She seemed to be speaking some words of gratitude to Hayley as they followed the crowd across the road to the sports club. I stumbled behind them feeling useless, invisible. Hayley was able to wrangle my brother when I couldn't. He had upstaged me, like he was deliberately trying to make me look useless.

At the wake, I spent most of my time outside, silently sipping vinegary wine from a plastic cup, only going back inside to refill it and notice that Hayley had gladly taken on the role of carer for the day. It has started to rain. I stood under the thin awning at the back of the building, smoking my cigarettes with a shaking hand.

Hayley found me.

'I thought you smoked Stuyvesants,' he said, taking one of my Marlboros from the pack and lighting one for himself without asking. 'Ann asked me to make sure you weren't passed out somewhere.'

'So you're my carer now? Who's watching Louis?' I stared out as the rain dripped from the sides of an old rusted cannon that was part of the grounds — a historical landmark of some kind — a pathetic, dull, relic of the past.

'You haven't heard from her, have you?'

I shook my head.

Hayley drained the bottle of beer in his hand and tossed it out onto the wet grass. 'I'm going to America in a few months.'

'Then even if I had heard from her, it wouldn't make any difference to you, would it?'

He stared at the burning cigarette between his fingers. His ears were red. 'I never hurt anyone, you know?'

I finished my wine and tossed the plastic cup in the same direction Hayley had thrown his beer bottle, hoping it would go further. I wanted to win. But the cup was so light the breeze lifted it briefly into the air before landing back at my feet; a sad drizzle of Shiraz dripping onto the toe of my shoe.

'I'm sorry about your mum,' I said, before walking back inside.

I scanned the room for Mother Ann. I needed to go home. I couldn't stand the crowd any longer. Someone tapped me on the shoulder. It was Melvin Clemence.

28 / THE VEIL

Melvin still prided himself on looking like Klaus Kinski. In *Aguirre: The Wrath of God*, Klaus Kinski plays a mutinous conquistador searching for the city of El Dorado and at one point he gets his hands on a baby sloth and as it twines its claws around his fingers, he explains that sloths are creatures that sleep their lives away. I thought, in the midst of my own slumber, that maybe it was an acceptable way to live. If one species can do it, why can't another adopt the same behaviour in order to survive?

I sat at Melvin's kitchen table. Waiting. Melvin told me she was coming, I just had to wait for a while. He somehow managed to avoid all my questions about where she was and what she was doing by saying that he really should let Laura fill me in on those details herself. He couldn't possibly intervene. When I asked him to at least tell me what prompted the sudden move, he shrugged and said:

'No idea. I was in Berlin, Jonathan never called me while I was over there, said he didn't want to pay for international calls. Cheap prick. I'm guessing he got a better job offer back in the city.' He had made me a cup of weak instant coffee and was talking relentlessly about Berlin. Something about spontaneous street theatre and Bertolt Brecht. After a while, he noticed I was tuning out. He got up to make himself another cup of coffee.

It all seemed wrong. Like I was in some kind of play, like there might be some kind of surveillance camera hidden above Melvin's fridge, like someone was watching me from far away and laughing

'Melvin…is she okay?'

'As okay as you appear to be,' he said, sitting down, crossing his legs and folding his arms in a slow, deliberate manner.

'How do I appear to be?' I asked.

'Alive but dead. Certainly unappealing.'

There was a knock on the door so loud it made the windows rattle. I stood up, looking around the room, unsure what to do. Melvin groaned and pulled the tufts of his (poorly bleached) blond hair behind each ear.

'Calm down, that'll just be Jade with Nina. Thought it might be good to reacquaint my daughter with her cousin.'

I heard some muffled, strained conversation before Melvin returned through the arched entrance to the kitchen. Nina pushed past him wearing a florescent yellow swimsuit and dragging a backpack twice her size.

'Mum let me have a swim before we came here,' Nina said to me, like she had just seen me yesterday. She climbed onto the chair next to me. 'You're my cousin,' she said, fiddling with a teaspoon in front of her.

'No,' I began, I'm —'

'She's your cousin Laura's friend,' said Melvin. 'She held you when you were a baby.'

'Yeah, I remember that. I'm six now. All my cousins are boys,' Nina snapped at her father.

'I'm Albert,' I said.

'I know,' said Nina.

'Bloody hell,' sighed Melvin under his breath, plonking a plastic cup full of apple juice in front of her.

Nina started to pick her nose. She rolled a ball of hard snot between her thumb and forefinger and ate it. 'He's not my dad,' she said, pointing a small finger at Melvin.

'Nina, I am your father, and believe me, I was there as the whole gory mess unfolded and don't you dare say you remember that too because you clearly don't.'

Nina ignored him. 'Mum is going to Amsterdam with Brett. I'm staying here. Can you take me shopping?'

'Brett is Jade's husband,' said Melvin. 'She married him almost the second I left for Berlin. He's Dutch.' He screwed his face up in disgust. 'I've only met him once, but the whole time he was talking to me he had this little bit of spittle on his lower lip that made me sick and now I can't get it out of my mind.'

'Is Jonathan coming too?' I asked.

Melvin said he wasn't sure.

'It was Val I spoke to on the phone. She just said they were coming up on Sunday and today is definitely Sunday. Listen, I have to quickly run into town and get some groceries. Do you think you can watch Nina for a little while?' He didn't leave me with much choice. He promised he'd be back by the time they arrived, whenever that was.

I lay on an old trampoline — likely the same one Laura had — in Melvin's back yard. Nina was jumping up and down next to me. Melvin had been gone an hour already. It was 2pm. Nina was complaining she wanted some lunch, but I kept telling her, her father would be back with food any second.

'He always buys two-minute noodles and soy milk. Sometimes he'll let me have an ice block.'

'Do you like your cousin Laura?' I asked.

She collapsed on her back next to me, as the trampoline's momentum slowed to the speed of a heaving lung.

'Yeah I do, I told you that already.' She noticed the confusion in my face. 'I just don't like talking to her very much because she's not nice to me all the time, but she can be fun when she feels like it. She is a woman of war.'

'What do you mean?'

'Daddy says when someone has been through a lot, they are a person of war. He says Mummy is not like that. Mummy doesn't know what war is like.' She inspected my face. 'Are you sick? Is that why you've been lying down instead of jumping?'

'Yeah,' I said. 'I'm sick all the time.'

'Get away from me then,' Nina said, diving off the trampoline and landing in a tangled mess on the grass.

I leaned over the edge and asked her if she was okay.

'I'm okay, I just want to stay like this for a while. It feels good. No breathing on me, I don't want to catch your sick.' Nina started making a strange grunting sound. I went back inside to watch her from the living room window. I imagined what would happen when Laura arrived:

The pigment around her eyes would be darker than usual, like she'd been awake all night, trying to decide whether it was a good idea to come and see me. She would hug me and she would smell like a mixture of men's cologne and sage. She would be wearing a pair of black jeans with a hole in one knee and a black knitted jumper that seemed to swallow her arms and torso. Fashionably ill-fitting. Her hair would no longer be black but a chocolate brown. It would fall just below her shoulders.

We would go into a room where we could talk, uninterrupted. I would ask her about her health. She would say she was attending group therapy at the local hospital, and it was going well, but she was on meds that took her appetite away. I would tell her mine did the opposite. I would tell her about Doctor Brunner — the simpering bastard — that I had lost all faith in shrinks. She would suggest instead that I write it all down, that I was always better at writing than speaking and she was better at speaking than writing. I would agree that these contrasting strengths worked in our favour, that if our minds were somehow combined, we would be indestructible.

Nina, having had enough of writhing about in the grass, came inside and sat down next to me. I had pulled some old photographs and letters from Laura out of my bag and was contemplating whether to share them with her when she arrived. Nina picked up a picture of Laura at about nine years old, sitting on her father's white sofa, her legs curled underneath her, head turned to the side as though she were preoccupied with something just out of view. I couldn't remember who took the photo, or how it ended up in my collection. It had just always been there.

'Who is this?' Nina asked.

'It's your cousin, can't you tell? You weren't born yet when it was taken but it's definitely her.'

'Which cousin?'

'Laura.'

'No, no,' Nina shook her head. 'All my cousins are boys.'

She asked me to turn the television on. It was the same style we owned in the eighties, with knobs on the side, covered in a dark wood veneer. An antenna sat on the top. I told Nina it didn't look like it worked any more. She told me it did, you just had to fiddle with the rabbit ears a bit. After cycling through every channel on the dial and moving the rabbit ears in various directions to pick up a signal, I finally found what looked like the community channel Laura and I would sometimes come across late at night. We particularly enjoyed watching the karaoke competition, but only got any amusement out of the most untalented, inebriated contestants. This time, there was some kind of current affairs show on, produced by high school students who wandered the streets of the city, a big fluffy microphone in hand, sticking it in the faces of passers-by.

'How do you feel about letting refugees into the country?' A squeaky-voiced boy in a back-to-front cap asked an elderly man.

'Should bloody well let the boats sink,' the man grumbled, 'because you can never be too sure with that lot, can you?'

Nina lay on her side, far too close to the screen. She yawned.

I must have fallen asleep because Nina shook me awake, telling me the TV had gone all fuzzy again and why wasn't her father home yet? She wanted to go and sit outside on the footpath to wait for Melvin, as if that would make him magically appear.

I opened Melvin's front gate, telling Nina that if we walked for a while it might pass the time. She took my hand and we slowly made our way down the dirt road. I turned back once and thought I saw a familiar shape, a shadow. It seemed to shift and distort itself, like the picture on an old videocassette.

'Who's that man?' Nina asked, shielding her eyes from the setting sun.

I told her there was no man. I knew that if I wanted to keep walking, I had to tell the most hideous lies.

AUTHOR'S NOTES

A version of this novel, titled *Laura Lives on Cloud Nine*, was submitted in 2019 for the award of Doctor of Creative Arts at the University of the Sunshine Coast. I have made some of my own alterations since, yet I would like to acknowledge Jane Todd for professional copy editing and proofreading advice on my thesis as covered in the Australian Standards for Editing Practice, Standards D and E. In turn, I would like to thank and acknowledge Professor Gary Crew and Dr Paul Williams for their supervision and guidance during the this time.

When I was close to completing my thesis, I received an autism diagnosis. Until that point, I was writing and researching *Laura* as – at least, in part – an exploration of mental illness. I do not wish to elaborate on any lived experience that went into this work, except to say that Albert was clearly autistic – she just didn't know it yet. I'm learning to love her. I hope anyone who lived through the latter decades of the twentieth century, diagnoses both early and late, now feel that they belong.

ACKNOWLEDGEMENTS

I would like to thank the following people; many of whom have been rightfully frustrated by my initial refusal to let this book rear its little dirt-encrusted head. No, I did not pursue traditional publication for this one, but next time. Next time.

To my parents for supporting all my non-lucrative decisions and letting me scream it out when I need to.

To my brother, Luke for the hugs and tissues. I am so very sorry for so many things, and so very proud of you.

To my women:

Krista: my sister back in St Olaf. Your empathy and strength is unmatched.

Rhiannon: a huge mole who always steps up and lets me explore the crude and craptacular.

Alison: You're one of my safe people, too.

Roxann: I'm sorry we were late for your wedding.

Shael: You gave me the final kick up the arse.

To James for being the first person to see I might be good at this. Thank you. Hope you're good.

To Gary, Ross and Paul, thank you for welcoming me back after so long.

To Oscar for being an eager and motivating early reader.

To the ghost of Shirley Jackson: guess what? I'm a witch now.

To Belle, Mena, Daisy, Audrey and Skye. All of you angels, all of you gods.